ALPHA'S PRIZE

A BILLIONAIRE WEREWOLF ROMANCE

RENEE ROSE
LEE SAVINO

Midnight
ROMANCE

COPYRIGHT

Published in the United States of America
    Renee Rose Romance and Silverwood Press

Editor: Miranda

This e-book is a work of fiction. While reference might be made to actual historical events or existing locations, the names, characters, places and incidents are either the product of the author's imaginations or are used fictitiously,

WANT FREE BOOKS?

Go to reneeroseromance.com to sign up for Renee Rose's newsletter and receive a free copy of *Theirs to Protect, Owned by the Marine, Theirs to Punish, The Alpha's Punishment, Disobedience at the Dressmaker's* and *Her Billionaire Boss.* In addition to the free stories, you will also get special pricing, exclusive previews and news of new releases.

Go to www.leesavino.com to sign up for Lee Savino's awesomesauce mailing list and get a FREE Berserker book —too hot to publish anywhere else!

1

S*edona*

MY EYES CRACK OPEN, gritty and sore. I'd rub them if I weren't in wolf form.

Where am I?

I rise and knock against metal bars. *Oh fates.* I'm in a cage—a *fucking cage.*

Now Sedona, my mom would say, lips pursed. *Do you really have to swear?*

Yes, mom. If ever there was a time for the 'f' word, this is fucking it.

I'm in a cage, like a fucking dog. A goddamn pet.

I rub my head against the bars, but that doesn't help the pounding pain. My mouth is dry and I fight to swallow around a serious case of cottonmouth. Worse than any hangover I've had in the last three years of college. Not that I'm a party girl or anything.

Well, sometimes I like to party, but who doesn't?

I twist in the confined space, but it's impossible to get comfortable. A low growl starts in my throat, and my wolf hunches down to pounce. I slam against the bars and whine in pain. A few more tries and I give up, slumping muzzle to paws, squeezing my eyes shut against the ache. My headache screams louder. My captors dosed me with something to knock me out. How long have I been floating in and out of consciousness? Twelve hours? Twenty-four?

I'm in a large warehouse. Other cages line a giant metal rack of shelves—like the kind products are stored on in Costco or Sam's Club. Most are empty. A skinny black wolf with yellow eyes blinks at me from where he lies on his side in one of them.

Cigar smoke tinges the air and the sound of men's voices, speaking in Spanish, comes from behind a door. It swings open, allowing a shaft of light to fall from the corridor. The masculine voices draw nearer until a group of men gather around my cage. The same assholes who grabbed me on the beach.

If I were smart, I'd shift and get some information out of them. Who they are, what they want with me. But my wolf doesn't feel like talking.

I surge to my feet, my back and head pressing against the top wires of my tiny prison. My lips peel back to show my fangs. A deadly growl rumbles in my throat.

"*Que belleza, no*?" one of the men asks.

There is more discussion in Spanish, but I don't catch any words, besides *Americana* and *Monte Lobo*.

They're wolves, judging by their scent. All of them. Their leers send a cold prickle of fear through me.

I snap my jaws through the wires, snarling.

Ignoring me, the men pick up my cage and carry me

outside to a gleaming white passenger van. They open the back doors of the van and lift me inside.

I throw myself against the wires of the cage, barking and growling.

One of the men chuckles. *"Tranquila, ángel, tranquila."* He swings the doors shut with a decisive click, leaving me alone once more.

~.~

I BOUNCE around the cage in the dark. The van seems to ascend, traveling over bumpier and bumpier ground—must be a dirt road. I shift back to human form to think, hunching naked between the bars.

My head is clearing from the sedative, although my stomach still roils like I just rode a double upside down loop roller coaster.

I need a plan. Some strategy to get the hell out of here. I grope the padlock on the outside of the cage. It's solid. I'd need wire cutters or a lock pick to get free, but I've got nothing. My older brother, Garrett, taught me how to pick locks. I watched him hell around as a teenager, picking every lock our dad tried to use to keep him in, or out, depending on the situation.

But I have no hairpin, no purse. Not a stitch of clothing.

Where are they taking me? My stomach knots. If this was a random kidnapping, I'd say I'd be ransomed back to my family. But I'm an alpha's daughter. Someone might have a bone to pick with my dad, in which case... I'm going to be gang raped by a foreign pack. Turned into their sex slave. Fates, I hope they're not into torture.

My wolf whines as the scent of my own fear clogs my nose.

Think, Sedona, think!

They're wolves. They picked me up off of a tourist beach in San Carlos. I'm young, female. They're probably not going to kill me. Female shifters are rarer than males. I'm a commodity. Maybe they're going to auction me off?

Fuck. This is bad. Very bad.

Garrett didn't like the idea of me going to San Carlos with humans. Like a fool, I blew off his concern. Thought he was being overprotective. I'm a shifter. What's the worst that can happen?

Turns out, a-fucking-lot. I can almost hear my dad saying, *I told you so.* If I get out of here alive, I'll happily agree.

The van rumbles to a stop. My wolf fights to take over, to protect me, but I force her back. My only play is to pretend to cooperate, then gouge their motherfucking eyes out with my thumbs and run. To act docile, it's better that I be naked and afraid, like the stupid reality show.

I roll to my side, pull my knees up and cover my breasts with my forearm. *There.* Helpless as a baby rabbit.

The van door opens.

"Please," I rasp. "I'm so thirsty."

One of the men mutters something in Spanish. Oh yeah. This game is going to be harder because I don't speak the language.

Damn, why didn't I take Spanish in high school? Oh right, because I wanted to be in every art class possible. And I had no idea I'd one day I'd have to speak with my Mexican kidnappers.

"Let me out of the cage," I plead, praying someone speaks English.

They ignore me. Two men pick my cage up by the handles on each side and carry it out of the van. They don't set it down, either. They walk up a tree-lined path, the cage jostling and swinging between them. Beyond the landscaped lawns and high-walled building, there's only thick woods. My captors brought me to a fortress on top of a mountain.

My pulse gallops into high gear. "Please," I beg. "I need water. And food. Let me out."

"*Cállate,*" one of them hisses. Even I know that word. I am from Arizona, after all. *Shut up.*

Okay, so they're less than sympathetic.

Two older men—also shifters, judging by their smell—dressed in Italian suits and shoes shined up like mirrors, emerge from behind a giant portcullis made of steel and carved wood.

Drug dealers.

That's my first thought, based on the way they're dressed, although if there was a shifter drug cartel, I would've heard of it. *Wouldn't I?* But who else wears thousand dollar suits on a wooded mountain?

The well-heeled men speak to my captors in low tones and usher them in.

I try my naked and afraid game again. "Please help me, *señor*. I'm so thirsty."

One of the older men turns and looks directly at me, and I know he understands. He says something in sharp tones to my captors, who mutter back.

Yeah, that didn't get me very far. But they have to open this cage sometime. And when they do, I'll be busting noses, shifting and getting the hell out of Dodge. No more nice wolf.

My stomach lurches as the cage sways. I have to clutch the metal rungs to keep from sliding with the movement.

The men follow a path along the inside of the high polished adobe walls. An enormous villa or mansion made of gleaming white marble rises up on the other side, majestic. It has an otherworldly quality, like we're in a completely different era. Or dimension.

We arrive at a modern security door and one of the older men pulls out a keycard. He opens the door and leads my captors inside and down a flight of steps. There's a damp coolness to the air. My nose wrinkles at the musty smell.

I blink as my eyes adjust to the dim lighting. Oh lordy. I'm in a dungeon. I swear to the fates, there are iron doors with peephole windows all along the corridor. One of the old men barks something in Spanish and they stop and set the cage down to wait for him to unlock a cell door.

The minute I see what's inside, I shift, my snarls echoing off the stone walls.

The room holds nothing but a bed with iron shackles attached to the four posts, ready to hold a prisoner. And now I know why they brought me here.

I throw myself against the cage walls. Somebody, somehow, is going to feel my fangs.

A sharp jab pricks my neck and my legs go out from under me again.

My growls echo in my ears as my vision fades once more to black.

~.~

Carlos

THE BACK of my neck prickles as Don Jose leads me down the marble steps of the palace.

"Where are we going?" My dress shoes click on the stone, echoing against the walls of the dimly lit passageway, which glow from being scrubbed and polished daily.

The head of *el consejo*, the council of elders, inclines his head. "We need you to see something." He keeps walking, expecting me to follow, like I'm still a clueless pup.

A low growl rises in my throat. Don Jose glances back and I swallow back my wolf's response.

"Calm your wolf, Alpha, if you would. You will want to see this." The slight deference in his words doesn't touch his arrogant tone. I grit my teeth until he takes the turn to descend into the dungeons—the holding area for enemy wolves and insurgents.

"Enough," I snap. My wolf's distrust is too intense to ignore. "What is it you're showing me?"

Don Jose hesitates.

"I'm not a pup anymore," I say softly. "I'm your alpha."

For a moment the old wolf's gaze meets mine. He drops it a second before it turns into a real challenge. "You know our birth rates have been falling these past few years."

"More like this past half a century," I correct.

"Indeed. And many of the births produce only *defectuosos*," Don Jose spits. "Weaklings, unable to shift. In days of old—"

I raise my chin, daring him to finish his point. I fucking hate the elders' *days of old* proclamations.

"In days of old, a shifter who has no animal is not a shifter," he says stiffly. "They were removed from the pack."

Removed. A nice way to say *killed.*

"You know my decision on this, Don Jose. Any wolf born to the pack is part of the pack. We do not turn our back on our own."

"Of course," he bows his head again, his back rigid as he scowls at a point on my tie. "But the pack must remain strong. Otherwise the weak blood will dilute us until no pup has the ability to shift at all."

"All right." I cross my arms over my chest. "Get to the point."

"The council has been working on a solution. While you were away at school, we had to make many difficult decisions. For the good of the pack."

"For the good of the pack," I murmur. "All right then. Show me."

I prowl behind Don Jose through the dimly lit passage.

"You'll see." Jose's dark eyes are cunning as he orders a guard to open the cell door.

The trouble is, I have no beta. I have Jose as part of *El Consejo,* the council of elders. I could easily best any of the individual members, but together, they are stronger than I am. The only reason they keep me as their puppet leader is because the pack law uses blood royalty to determine alpha. Someone from the original alpha bloodline bears the name of alpha, even if he doesn't rule like one.

The cell door swings open and I freeze.

Cuffed spread-eagle on a bed lies a beautiful, naked female. Her long, thick brown hair fans out around her head on a pillow-less mattress. Lush breasts, a flat tummy, legs that go on for a mile. And between them—ah, *carajo*—a perfectly waxed mound and her tender pink center on display for all to see.

What the actual fuck? A kick of heat flashes through me, thickens my cock. My hands curl to fists. My wolf is howling, adrenaline pumping through my veins, but I don't know if it's preparing me to claim the gorgeous female or fight for her freedom.

The woman strains against her bonds, the whites of her huge blue eyes flashing. Her full lips are chapped and bleeding. When she whimpers, red hot fury kicks through me. The need to protect her, to rescue her from this predicament, shoves to the surface, erasing all traces of my ill-timed lust.

"What in the hell is this?" I stalk forward and catch one of her cuffed wrists, yanking on the chain. "Unbind her," I thunder.

Later, I'd replay the scene over and over again, berating myself for my stupidity. A sinister chuckle is all I hear before I whirl to see the heavy door swing closed, locking with a resounding clang.

Rage makes me shift in a flash, shredding my tailored clothing midair as I launch toward the door, my huge wolf body hitting it at full force, but not budging it even a millimeter. I snarl, leaping about the room, my fury too great for rational thought as I snap and growl, prowling the perimeter, searching for any way to escape. Of course there's none. I know these cells well.

Shit.

I turn back to the girl. Oddly, despite my ferocious display of fury, her blue eyes don't hold panic now. She watches me with avid interest. Maybe because we're in the same boat—two prisoners left to... *damn.*

I know what they want.

Somehow, they've found a she-wolf from another pack and they kidnapped her to use for breeding. I knew they wanted me to mate but I had no idea they'd go this far.

I will kill them all—tear their damn throats out, every single one of the *pinche* council members. Holding me—their alpha—against his will, to be used as a goddamn stud?

Fuck no.

I roar and throw myself against the door one more time, though I know it's useless. Remembering a camera should be in the corner, I leap at it, clamping my fangs down on the smooth plastic and crushing the glass lens between them.

Fuck. Them.

I circle the small cell again and return to the bed, where I clamp my jaws down on the chain that holds one of the girl's wrists.

She closes her delicate hand into a fist, keeping her fingers away from my teeth.

Fates, her scent.

She smells like...heaven. Sugar cookies and almonds with a touch of citrus. And wolf. This female sure as hell isn't *defectuosa*. I wonder what her wolf looks like. Black, like mine? Grey? Tan?

I give my head a shake. It doesn't matter. I'm not mating her. I'm getting her the hell out of here.

I growl and pull with all my might, tear at the damn chain to pull it out of the wall.

The gorgeous female joins in, her youthful muscles bulging in a show of spectacular athleticism. The two of us heave together with all our might, but the chain doesn't pull free.

I sink on my haunches.

"Thanks for trying." Her American English contains a sweet, musical lilt.

No. I'm not interested in this enticing American, no matter how charming and beautiful she may be. That's what they want.

They think if they throw me in here with her, I'll claim the prize they caught for me. Sink my teeth into her and mark her forever. They're relying on my alpha instinct to mate another alpha and reproduce.

Do they think I'll forgive or forget this manipulation? Do they seriously think I'll let any of them live after this stunt?

I shift back to human form.

Carajo. Now I, too, am naked, my clothes shredded from the shift. And this raging hard-on isn't going to make the beauty in chains feel any safer.

I whirl to turn my back to the bed. Well, hell. Of course my cock is harder than stone. No matter how pissed I am or how much I want to rescue her, chained beauty is undeniably the most erotic sight I've ever witnessed.

"Fuck." I pick up the tattered remains of my trousers and find my boxers within them. They're torn, but might stay on if I sort of hang onto them. I step into them.

"You speak English." There's a note of relief in her voice.

I scowl. She shouldn't trust me. Because if she knew what I want to do to that luscious, naked, *fully available* body of hers, she'd be screaming.

My shirt lies a few feet away. I grab it and brace myself against her intoxicating presence before I turn back.

It doesn't help. She's as beautiful as I thought. No— more. Somehow I make it to the side of the bed to arrange my shirt over as much of her skin, which is a shade of burnished gold with tan lines in the shape of what must have been a miniscule string bikini. My mouth waters imagining what she must have looked like on the beach where she earned her tan. I know she filled out her bikini in a way that made every male in the area groan.

I drape the fabric over her pussy and stretch the other end up toward her breasts.

She quakes, her thighs straining against the iron manacles on her ankles and I catch the scent of her arousal.

Fates, is that all it takes? A single brush of fabric against her most sensitive bits and she's already ripe for the taking?

I seriously will not survive this test.

Arranging the shirt becomes a torture in itself, because when the scent hits my nostrils, I yank the fabric too high and expose her pussy, then slide it off her breasts when I give it an impatient jerk down.

The way her nipples rise and fall with her quickened breath doesn't help matters, nor does those big blue eyes fixed on me.

"For fuck's sake," I mutter, stretching both ends simultaneously. My fingers brush her skin and I barely bite back a growl of excitement. It's baby soft. Smooth. My cock strains eagerly toward her and, like an idiot, I inhale deeply. The smell of her pheromones and arousal makes me dizzy. Judging by her scent, she's close to ovulation—they must've known that. Must've known that no full-blooded shifter male could survive being locked up with a naked alpha she-wolf in heat over the full moon without claiming her at the very least, if not marking her forever his.

I manage to cover her pussy and one breast with my shirt before I drop the fabric and step back. One more brush of her skin and I swear I'll be pawing every inch of her.

I somehow drag my eyes away from her uncovered breast, with its peach-tipped nipple beaded up and hard. I wonder which part of this scenario turns her on—the bondage, nudity, or my attention on her fucking gorgeous body. No, I definitely don't want to know.

My breath grows short as a fresh shot of lust kicks through me. I clear my throat. "You're American?"

She nods. "Are you?" Her voice comes out half-whisper half-croak and she clears it and runs her pink tongue along her chapped lips.

I bite back a groan.

Fates know I want to lie and say *yes*. Pretend I've been kidnapped from America, like her. Brought to Monte Lobo and thrown in a cell. Rage at my own predicament almost brings on another shift.

"No." I reach out to twitch the fabric up again, but only succeed in making it slide away from both breasts.

Fuck—those nipples. They are begging to be in my mouth, my tongue treating them to the adventure of a lifetime.

I close my eyes and pace away a few steps to master my lust. "Are you hurt?" It comes out gruffer than I mean it to.

"I'm thirsty."

I go to the door and pound my palm against it, making thunder of the steel echo against the walls of our cell.

I'm not surprised when there's no answer. "She needs water," I shout in Spanish. I can't see out the window because it's a one-way glass, frosted on the inside. This time I hear a low voice behind the door. Motherfuckers. They're standing there listening to this whole thing. At least I disabled the fucking camera.

"My name is Carlos. Carlos Montelobo." I steel myself once more to face her. "I am so sorry you've been mistreated this way."

She licks her lips again. She has to stop doing that. "It's not your fault."

That's where she's wrong, and I'm an asshole if I don't tell her.

Her eyes travel down from my face to my naked torso, reaching my waist before they skip back to my face. She blushes.

Oh fates. So sweet. So fucking sweet.

I stab my fingers through my hair. "Unfortunately, it is my fault."

Her eyes narrow.

I hold up my hands. "I mean, I didn't know they were doing this, but this is my pack. I'm supposed to be the fucking alpha. Only I was locked in with you by the council of elders."

"Why?"

She knows why. I can tell by the way her gaze darts to my erection.

I swallow and sit down on the bed, my focus traveling once more to her bonds, as if I might discover some other way to free her. "Our pack suffers from too much in-breed-ing. We've dwindled in size and many of our numbers are unable to even shift. We call them *defectuosos*. Most females are barren and cannot reproduce. I knew *el consejo* was working on a plan to introduce new breeding, but I had no idea it would be this." I jab a hand in the air to indicate the cell.

"They want you to breed with me?"

"Yes." Guilt drops down on my chest like an anchor, dragging me into its depths.

Her cheeks grow pink and she pulls at her chains.

"Shh." I touch her before I realize my own intent, stroking her cheek with my thumb. "Don't worry, beautiful. I won't force myself on you, I promise." When she continues to tug on her bonds, I grip both her wrists below the shackles. *"Stop."* My voice sharpens with command.

She freezes, her wolf responding instinctively to the dominance of an alpha male. Her glare doesn't match her obedience, though.

And her body's response doesn't match the stink eye.

Yeah, my body is right there with hers. Restraining her has my cock waving like a flag. Her exquisite breasts are just inches from my chest. I can feel the heat of her body, the puff of her breath against my neck.

"I don't want you to hurt yourself any more than you've already been harmed." I ease my weight from her and release her wrists.

She flushes, and I want to tear out my own throat when tears pop into those incredible blue eyes. One escapes and slides down her cheek. I reach out to thumb it away. "Don't cry, *muñeca*. I won't claim you and I won't let them hurt you. You have my word."

She jerks her face away from my hand. "Why should I trust you?"

She's smart. "You shouldn't."

I'm not even certain I can honor my word, but I know I will die trying. "Right." She gives a bitter laugh.

2

*C*ouncil Elder

I STAND OUTSIDE the cell with my fellow elders Don Jose and Don Mateo, watching the two young wolves interact. I've sent the guards away. They aren't necessary—these cells are impossible to break out of. "It's only a matter of time. Their attraction is already apparent."

"Agreed," Mateo says. "He'll mark her before midnight. That much of the plan will be successful. But when we let him out, he may rip all our throats out. His wolf has grown fierce since we saw him last."

"I have a plan for that." Don Jose taps one finger on the door. "We drug them both before we separate them, then overdose his mother. When Carlos wakes, he will have to respond to that crisis first. He'll forget his fury because his mother will require all the gentleness he has inside him."

"That's not much of a plan," Mateo says.

"By the time he finds his female again, she'll be locked in a guest room, dressed in fine robes and being treated like royalty. He'll have no cause to punish us for our means, as he'll be pleased with the result—a beautiful prize for a strong alpha. Just what this pack has needed. Of course, we'll humbly beg his forgiveness."

I narrow my eyes. "It's risky. What if he lets her go?" Although I was the one who the traffickers notified when they kidnapped the American she-wolf, the idea to imprison her with our alpha was Don Jose's. I would have preferred *in vitro* fertilization. To use the girl as a breeder for the entire pack. A science experiment. We can't depend on nature or animal nature to keep the pack healthy.

"If he marks her, he won't be able to let her go. Biology will take its course, just as it will tonight."

"You're sure of it." I say it more like a statement than a question.

"Yes."

Juanito, a nine-year-old servant, arrives with the water I instructed him to fetch. He's a slight risk, because he's Carlos' favorite, but that's also why I picked him. We need someone to deliver food and drink to the couple, and I don't trust Carlos not to tear off the hand that goes through the window. He won't hurt the boy, though. There's too much goodness in him. Just like his father.

Which was why we had to get rid of him.

~.~

Sedona

. . .

CARLOS PACES AWAY from me and I register the loss of his closeness like a plant deprived of water. Which pisses me off. I don't want to be so turned on by the dark, brooding, mostly naked alpha stalking around our cell. Even if he is made of solid muscle so sculpted he could be a bodybuilder. I watch him, fascinated. His chest is hairless and a tattoo covers his left shoulder and biceps, some sort of geometric pattern. A second tattoo covers his right biceps.

I've never had such a strong reaction to any male— human or shifter. But then again, I've never been chained with my naked body on full display for a male, either.

I replay the scene where he held me down to make me stop pulling on my manacles. He moved lightning-fast, pouncing over me, pinning me to the bed. For one second, I thought he was going to kiss me. *Damn.* He has neatly trimmed facial hair. What would it feel like against my skin?

What would it be like to have my wrists pinioned over my head by him while he plowed into me? To have all that command and power focused on me. Would he make it hurt? Or is he a tender lover?

Even though his high-handedness annoyed me, he was right to stop me. My wrists are already bruised from where I pulled and the silliest part of me loves that he flexed his will for my own good. It's what a good alpha should do.

A square window at the base of the heavy door slides back and a small hand pushes a plastic tumbler through.

Carlos springs into action, diving for it, but instead of taking the tumbler, he grabs the wrist delivering it.

"*Ay!*" The cry of pain from the other side sounds distinctly childlike.

Carlos curses. "Juanito?"

"*Perdóname, Don Carlos.*" The boy sounds like he's about to cry.

Carlos lets out a string of Spanish curses, many of which I recognize. He demands something in Spanish but the boy only answers with a sniffle. Carlos releases his wrist and says something in more soothing tones. The small hand folds up and bumps Carlos' fist before it retreats. Carlos picks up the tumbler of water and stalks toward me. A tightly-leashed fury radiates from him, which I find oddly attractive. But yeah, I was raised by a dominant, generally pissed-off alpha wolf, so I guess that would be my male ideal. It actually makes sense why no other male has caught my interest until now. My wolf only shows her belly to a true alpha.

Great. I hope there's therapy for this, because the last thing I need is another big shot male telling me what to do. I already have an over-protective father and brother for that.

I watch his muscles ripple as he walks to the side of the bed.

"They send a boy with the water because they know I won't hurt him. *Chingada bola de pendejos.*"

"Who is the boy?" I'm thinking he's a relative of Carlos.

"A servant."

"Don't they have child labor laws in Mexico?"

Carlos' expression darkens even more. "I know. My pack is... archaic. They—*we*— his voice takes on a bitter tone— "live in a different era. The weak serve the strong. And they're kept weak by design. Congress or commerce with outsiders is forbidden, technology and media is not allowed, nor do we even trade with other packs. Only the council and myself are exempt from all these rules."

Water sloshes over the lip of the purple plastic tumbler. With far greater finesse than he showed when he tried to cover me with his shirt, he slides a hand behind my head and lifts it to meet the cup. I guzzle down half the water, not even caring that some of it dribbles down my chin. "Thank you," I gasp when I'm finished.

"If you don't approve, why don't you change things?"

A muscle in his jaw jumps. "I am—I will. It's a fight—always a fight against the council. But I will."

I accept another sip of water from the tumbler.

Carlos stares down at me with glittering dark eyes. "I don't even know your name."

"Sedona."

He raises a brow. "Like the city?"

"My parents met there." A few years ago, I was afraid Sedona and Tucson would be the farthest I'd ever travel from my home pack in Phoenix. And now I'm somewhere in Mexico, chained to a bed with a sexy Latino wolf devouring my naked body with his eyes. Not quite the adventure I'd hoped for.

Carlos repeats my name in his Spanish accent, giving it an exotic and sexy sound. "Beautiful name for a beautiful wolf." The fact that he finds me beautiful seems to piss him off, because he scowls when he says it. He lifts his hand to my mouth, like he's going to wipe the water off my chin, then retracts it with a grimace.

"Gee, thanks," I say drily.

He brings his thumb to my lower lip and rubs it, back and forth slowly, his dark eyes growing black.

A thrum starts between my legs and my nipples tighten.

Oh shit.

I'm totally out of my depth here. The honest truth—I'm a virgin. My dad would've killed any boy I screwed around with when I was in high school. And I mean that literally. I didn't even have a date to prom. I could've had sex in college, but I hang out with humans, and human males just don't ring my bell. Not that they haven't tried. I've messed around a little bit, but no intercourse.

The next thing I know, Carlos pushes his thumb between my lips and I'm making love to it with my tongue. A low growl reverberates in his chest like the start of an engine and all my lady parts rev up in response.

"Sedona," he rasps in his sexy accent again. *Say-doh-na.* He pronounces my name like it's a magical place. He drags his thumb from the suction of my mouth as if it pains him. "Being locked in here with you is going to kill me."

It must be the repeated tranquilizers they gave me because I'm seriously about to invite him to try out the Sedona buffet, seeing as how I'm all spread out here for his delight.

"What's your—" I clear my throat because I find it hard to speak now since he invaded my mouth with his thick digit — "What's your plan, exactly? Wait it out? I don't think that's going to work. If they locked you in here to get us to breed, will they let us out before we do?"

A muscle ticks in his jaw. He's beautiful angry, a lock of thick dark hair falling across his forehead, the strong lines of his face accented by the firm set of his mouth. His fingers close into fists at his side. "I don't know yet."

If I didn't have an alpha father and brother I might miss the legions of guilt and frustration coming off him in waves. Alphas can't stand not taking action, not having an answer, or having their hands tied. Considering the way his cock is locked in the upright position, the action he's most likely to take is thrusting into my warm, wet pussy. Not that I'm totally against the idea. Liquid trickles between my thighs as I fight to keep my head.

"How long have you been alpha?" I ask.

He rubs the back of his neck. "De facto—since my father's death when I was sixteen. But *el consejo* encouraged me to leave, to continue at my boarding school education and then to attend university in the United States. And then to go to graduate school. I didn't return until this fall." There's a heaviness to his words. I sense the weight of more guilt, or some other burden as he stares at the wall opposite him.

"You didn't want to return."

"No." He meets my eyes in a new way, as if the cloud of lust has lifted and he actually sees me, Sedona, not my naked body offered up on a platter. "I've never admitted that before. Even to myself."

"How long have you been gone?"

"Seven years. Long enough to comprehend if we don't make changes to this archaic place, the pack will die out."

I shudder. I'm the solution his council cooked up to save the pack. There's a certain amount of duty I was prepared for as an alpha's daughter. Being a part of a breeding program wasn't one of them. My dad is old school, but this is positively primeval.

He sits on the edge of the bed near my waist and examines the locks on my shackles. My wrists must look as raw as they feel because he rubs my skin around the edges of the cuffs and growls. "Tell me how you ended up here, Sedona."

The dominant tone makes me shiver. It doesn't matter that he's trying to be a gentleman. My body responds to him. "It's my spring break—or was. I was in San Carlos with my friends and a shifter approached me on the beach. Another came up behind me and stabbed a needle in my neck to drug me. They put me in a cage and flew me to a city where I spent the night in a warehouse. Then they drove me here."

Carlos growls through my entire story, while his

thumb works magic on the inside of my wrist, tracing light circles on my sensitive skin. I never realized a touch on the wrist was so sexy. My pussy throbs in a way that's hard to ignore. The strange heat floods my system again.

"Traffickers," he says when I finish. "From Mexico City. I'd heard a rumor that shifters were selling wolves in my country, but I didn't believe it. The stories feature a demon called the Harvester who buys shifters, drains their blood, and steals their organs."

I shudder.

"When we get out, I'll kill every last one of the traffickers who touched you. You have my word on that."

I swallow and nod. "Thank you."

He brushes his lips over my pulse. "Tell me, where do you go to school and what do you study, Sedona?"

I lick my lips to wet them, and his gaze snaps to my mouth. Fates, I may actually be blushing. I've had attention from males my entire life and never had this reaction. Shifting my hips to relieve the tickle between them, I answer, "I go to the University of Arizona, in Tucson. I'm getting a degree in commercial art."

He tilts his head to the side as if I've said the most fascinating thing on Earth. "An artist. *Claro que si.*"

"What does that mean?"

He smiles, shifting his attention to my other wrist. "*Yes, of course.* I should have known a wolf as beautiful as you would only put more beauty into the world."

I roll my eyes.

"What kind of art do you produce?"

I nibble my lip. "Right now I'm really into watercolors with black ink outlines."

"Like landscapes?"

I don't know why it embarrasses me to say what I've been drawing. I say it, anyway. "Fairies."

He cocks his head, studying me. I wait for him to scoff, but instead he asks, "Why fairies?"

"Um." I flush. No one's ever asked me this much about my art before. Not even my folks. "When I was little, I had a nanny. Well, an older wolf who watched me in the afternoon sometimes. She always told me if I took a nap when she wanted me to, good fairies would come and fill my life with magic. I, um, remember trying to draw them." I rush to finish my lame story, but he doesn't interrupt or look bored. "Later, when she got sick, I made her little cards decorated with fairies. Somehow, I never grew out of it."

"I would very much like to see your fairies, Sedona."

His intense gaze makes my heart flutter. I look away. "I don't really show them to anyone," I mumble.

"Why not?"

"My professors would think it's dumb. My folks think that art is just a phase I'm going through. Something cute for me to occupy my time with until I'm mated. It's like they sent me for the 1950s Mrs. degree."

Carlos clucked. "They should be proud of you, and leave you to your art."

"Yeah. My dad and brother just care about keeping me safe and protected. The rest doesn't matter so much."

"But only you can live your life. You should be free to make your choices."

I snort. "I've never been free. They're... dominant." I remember just in time not to mention that Dad and Garrett are both alphas. "Don't dominant wolves like making decisions for others?"

"An alpha should be a leader, yes." Carlos nods. He caught what I didn't say, and I should be worried, but all I can think is *smart wolf.* "He should oversee the good of the pack, protect the weak, and keep them safe. But he should also know what his members care about, what makes them tick. That is leadership."

I swallow hard. This is dangerous territory. At least Carlos doesn't seem to think all women should be tied to their beds for an alpha asshole to ravish and breed. Or he does, and he's talking a good game to manipulate me. I'm just not sure.

"What about you?" I redirect the conversation. "Where did you go to school?"

"Stanford for undergrad, Harvard for my MBA."

Wow. Okay, he *is* a smart wolf. No wonder he didn't want to come back to his pack. A spark of anger on his behalf kindles in my chest. He should be able to choose his own future, not be shackled to this crazy pack.

But a more pressing and disturbing thought pushes its way to the forefront of my mind. "Carlos? I have to pee."

~.~

CARLOS

MY WOLF LOVES the way Sedona looks up at me and spills her problem, like I'm the guy who will know how to fix it.

And then I'm enraged. There's a toilet in the room, but my female is *chained to a bed*. Yes, I called her *my female*. I know I can't keep her, but in this moment, she's under my protection. She's naked and vulnerable and—*mine.* My wolf snaps his teeth with that assertion. Down, boy.

I stomp to the door and pound on it again. "Give me the keys to her cuffs. Now."

I hear low voices murmuring behind the door, then Don Jose makes an offer, "The keys for the clothing."

Fuck. Me.

Anger has the cords in my neck standing out, but I'm impotent to act. I grit my teeth and turn to Sedona. "They say they will trade the keys for the scraps of clothing."

Her nostrils flare, lower jaw juts out at a stubborn angle. "Right. Because they're hoping for sexy time. How sexy will it be when I wet the bed?"

I can't hold back the bark of laughter that comes flying out. It surprises me—I honestly can't remember the last time I laughed. It's been years. Probably since before my father died.

Sedona's lips turn up into a wry grimace and I get lost in the cerulean blue of her eyes. And then, because there's no fucking way I'm letting my female be humiliated by wetting the bed, I make the decision for her. I march over and snatch my shirt from her body.

"Hey," she protests, but her nipples bead up.

"Your freedom is worth my discomfort," I tell her, dropping my boxers to the floor.

"*Your* discomfort?" Disbelief crowds her tone.

"Yes, *muñeca.* I'm the one who has to fight my instincts."

She blushes like an innocent, and I wonder how much sexual experience she has. She's mature, but still young.

It doesn't matter. She shouldn't be locked up with a wolf like me.

I gather up the other scraps littered around the room and give the delivery door a sharp kick. It slides back and I stuff the items through. Juanito's hand appears with the key. His wrist is still marked with red imprints from my fingers and guilt slams through me.

Of all the shifters in the hacienda, Juanito is one I would never wish to hurt. Juanito and my mother, may the fates protect her.

I wanted to ask Juanito to slip me the key to her cuffs when he delivered the water—I know the boy would do anything I ask—but I couldn't put him in that position. He'd get a terrible beating at best. At worst, *el consejo* would exact their revenge on his mother, and she's had enough grief in this lifetime after losing her husband to the mines and her eldest son disappearing.

If I can find a way to communicate with him alone, maybe he can get me the key to the door and I'll be out in time to protect him and his mother. Fates, how I'd like to just remove him from this dark place.

I take the key and Juanito's other hand appears with a ripe mango, still in its peel. I roll my eyes. Seriously? It's like they're taking advice from a bad dating book. *Eating a mango can be sensual and stimulating in foreplay. Lick the juice from your lover's skin, or have her suck on the seed.*

I take the fruit. My she-wolf may be hungry. I fist bump with Juanito again, stride back to the bed and unlock Sedona's wrist cuffs. She groans as she pulls her arms down and shakes them. When I've freed her ankles, I help her sit and rub her arms to get the life back in them.

"What is *moon-yeca*?" she asks.

I smile. "Doll."

"Oh." Her cheeks color again and she surges to her feet. "Turn around. I need some privacy."

"It's yours, doll." I stand up and walk to the other side of the room, turning my back to the toilet and biting the peel of the mango to tear a piece off.

The toilet flushes and I turn back. Sedona pours a bit of water from the cup over her hands to wash. My cock thickens at this new view of her. She's a goddess. Long legs, breasts, a perfect handful, her coppery brown hair falling in waves down her slender back.

And that ass...

In less than a minute, I could have Sedona on her hands and knees, spreading those ass cheeks wide for me as I hold a fistful of her silky hair and pound into her. She's hot for it. I could make her want it. It wouldn't even be rape...

I shake my head and swallow the growl starting up my throat, but not before she catches it.

She turns and quirks her brows. "What?" Then her gaze drops to my erect and bobbing cock and she knows what.

I don't know what I expected—another blush, or irritation. Maybe defensiveness. Instead, my American doll moistens her lips with her tongue.

I groan. "Don't do that, *muñeca*. Not unless you want to find out what it's like to be thrown face down on that mattress and fucked until you scream."

Her eyes widen and I know I went too far. Maybe I was trying to piss her off, to get her to put up a wall to keep me out. Because fates know my control is crumbling.

I face the wall so she doesn't have to look at my dick waving around while I speak with blatant vulgar disrespect.

And then it hits me—the scent of her arousal—so pure, so undeniable, my vision tunnels.

Fuck. My wolf wants to mark her. I haven't even kissed the female and he's ready to mate for life.

My fingernails turn to claws. I dig them into the wall and drag downwards, relishing the pain. Less than an hour and my control is dangerously close to breaking. I seriously don't know how I'll survive the night.

"Are you all right?" Her soft voice does wicked things to my body.

"Fine," I give a strangled chuckle. "Just fine."

"You don't seem fine."

"Just... give me a moment." I press my forehead against the wall. The council is smarter than I give them credit for. Locking me in with a female in heat—it's too much.

"Are... are you moon mad?" she asks.

"No." *Not yet.* I lean one hand against the wall. I'm dying to stroke my cock, just beat off right here to keep from marking her. I'd do it, except I doubt it'd help. "What do you know about moon sickness, Sedona?"

"I know dominant wolves get it when their wolf needs to mate and they deny him."

"Not just mate. *Mark.* For life."

"Have you ever had it?"

"No. If I did... I'd take a mate. Not like this," I hasten to explain. "I'd woo her. Court her. She'd have a choice. Of course."

"Your council doesn't take the same stance on she-wolves' rights."

"No," I breathe out, grateful she doesn't lump me in with them. "They don't. They've been pushing me to take a mate. But I'm not ready."

"Still playing the field?" Her tone has an edge that makes me turn. I brace as her beauty hits me like a blow.

"Jealous?" I try to joke. My voice comes out strangled.

She bites her lip.

"*Madre de Dios*," I mutter. "Don't do that."

Her lovely eyes widen. "Do what?"

"Nothing." I don't want to scare her. It's not her fault

she's perfect. "I'm not a player, no matter what you've heard about Latin lovers. I've never even had a she-wolf—only human females."

"I've never been with a wolf, either."

My fist curls at the thought of another male—wolf or human—touching her. I press my body against the wall and dig my nails into my palm until the bite makes me grit my teeth.

"You're in pain." The concern in her voice wraps around me.

And she's been kidnapped, drugged, and locked in a room to serve against her will in a bogus breeding program. I don't deserve her compassion.

"Look, Carlos. Neither of us want to be in this situation, but..."

I open my eyes. She's gnawing that lip again. Naughty she-wolf. I'd punish her for being a tease, if she were mine.

"Maybe I can do something to help you—" She lowers her eyes in the direction of my cock, flushing. I bite back a laugh. If I had known such an alluring innocent existed, I would have torn apart the world to find her.

"I mean," Sedona continues, "We're obviously attracted to each other—"

The roaring in my ears is the sound of all the blood in my body rushing to my cock. It's so loud I nearly miss her next comment, "We could just, I don't know, fool around." She shrugs and swallows. "It doesn't have to mean anything, beyond tonight."

I'm across the room before I realize my control has snapped. Sedona retreats, her face white at the wolf in my eyes. I stalk her until her back hits the wall and then plant my hands beside her head, caging her. I lean close, careful not to touch, but it's no use. Her sweet scent makes me dizzy.

"Is that what you did with your little humans? Fool around?" My voice comes out a growl.

"No," she breathes. Her pupils are blown.

I curl a lock of her hair around my index finger. "No? You sure, *ángel*? Because I seriously want to kick the ass of every *boy* who's ever touched you." I've gone way too far, but I can't seem to dial back the competitive aggression burning just below the surface now.

She shoves at my chest and when I don't move, tries to duck under my arm.

Yeah, I definitely went too far.

"Wait." I catch her and pull her back. "I'm sorry. I know I'm being an asshole."

"Yeah. You are."

I flip her around, hold her against me until she stops struggling. Her scent envelops me, and I know she really is an angel. I'm in heaven. My lips nuzzle her ear. "I'm trying. You see how difficult this is for me..." I rub my cock against her bare rear.

Her breath grows ragged. "I know. I can help with that."

"Thank you, Sedona." Although it pains me, I release her. "But I don't think that's a good idea."

She hides the hurt confusion on her face. "Whatever." She stalks to the bed and sits down, arms crossed over her chest.

"You can't seriously think I don't want you." My goddamn dick bobs in front of me as nodding in agreement.

She gives a shrug.

"No, I mean for me, there's no fooling around. Not with you. Because I wouldn't be satisfied with just one night."

She shakes her head, muttering something about men and overinflated opinions of their stamina.

"One night wouldn't be enough because I'd want more of you. Not sex. Not fooling around. *You.*" I take a deep breath and tell her the truth. "If my wolf was ready to choose a mate, I'd choose a she-wolf like you."

"What?"

"Kind. Intelligent. Educated."

A smile plays over her lips. "You forgot smoking hot."

"*Muñeca,* I didn't forget."

She laughs and her breasts bounce lightly. My cock is so hard I'm in pain. But I'd give anything to see her laugh again.

I sit next to her, leaving a space between us. My heart stops racing when I get a lungful of her scent. My wolf seems content I'm with my female. Maybe I can do this.

I bump her shoulder with mine. "I changed my mind. Let's fool around."

"Don't make fun of me."

"I'm not. I would never." I search for a peace offering, and remember the mango. "Are you hungry?" Retrieving the fruit, I tear off a piece. She reaches for it and I shake my head. *You want to play, doll? Let's see how you handle this game.*

I bring the mango to her lips. She holds onto the stiffness in her body for another moment, then leans forward to bite into the ripe yellow flesh. As expected, the fruit dribbles down her chin and neck, dropping onto her chest in sticky rivulets. "Oh my God," she exclaims with her mouth full, hands flying up to catch the juice. She chews, moaning. "This is so good. Mangoes are not this good in the States."

"It's fresh. We have a grove inside the hacienda walls with all kinds of fruit-bearing trees—almond, avocado, lemon, lime, sapote, papaya."

"Mmm." She leans forward and takes another bite. "This is one reason I've always wanted to travel. The food."

"You haven't traveled?" I peel a new section, smiling like a fool as she lets me feed her.

She licks her lips and my vision darkens. The only thing keeping me from claiming her is my satisfaction watching her eat. My wolf is content, for now.

"I always wanted to get out, see the world. My folks won't let me. They're protective."

"With good reason," I say softly and feed her another bite.

"I used to think being named after an Arizona town was a curse. Like I'd never get to leave. Of course, my one trip ended with me here—" She waves a hand at the cell.

"You will get out of here safely, Sedona. You'll get your chance to travel. You have my word."

"Thanks." She swallows and forces a smile. "Until then, I'm just going to pretend I'm stuck at a second-hand resort with an unfortunate dungeon theme. Of course, the food service here is very hands on." She waggles her brows. A joke. Stuck in this hellhole with me, and she's making a joke. She's... *incredible*.

I can't stop myself from leaning down and kissing the side of her mouth. I pull back immediately, but her taste lingers on my lips, a bit of mango sweetness. "Forgive me, I... you had something." I gesture to her face.

"Like I said," she grins. "Very hands on."

At a loss for words, I raise the mango again. She eats like she's ravenous, devouring the tender flesh. I make quick work of the peel, dropping it at our feet and turning the sticky fruit around and around until she's eaten all the orange meat. "Sorry. I didn't save you any."

"I'm fine, *muñeca*. Do you want the seed?" I'm dying as I

offer it to her. She's winning this game without even trying. I won't survive the torture of watching her suck the seed, and yet every cell in my body *requires* I see it.

She lifts her brows. "What do you do with it?"

There. It's all over. I have to show her. I push the seed between her lips, fuck her mouth with it.

Her eyes dilate, teeth clamp down and scrape the remaining flesh from the seed. I pull the seed out so she can swallow and she sounds breathless.

Fates take me now.

Her pretty pink tongue extends from her mouth to lick away some of the juice from her lips. "Don't think I don't know what you're doing."

"What am I doing?" My voice is pure gravel.

"Making love to me with a mango."

I thrust the seed back between her lips. "No, beautiful. *That* wasn't making love to you with a mango." I pull the seed back out and trail it down her neck, between her breasts. I follow with my mouth, licking along the sweet trail of juice I've left. "*This* is making love to you with a mango."

I drag it all the way down her belly, turn the seed flat side up and rub between her legs.

She cries out and tries to close her thighs but I make a sharp disapproving sound and she stills.

Fates, I'm really doing this.

She whimpers, rocking her pelvis down to grind into the fruit. We both pant as I rub it back and forth over her slit, her juices mingling with the mango's. The sound is slick, like sex. I pull the mango seed away and bring it back with a slap, spanking her pussy. Her eyes widen and she emits a needy moan.

"Do you need me to clean up my mess, baby?" I slap her with the mango seed again. Our eyes are locked, and I'm hoping she'll see I've reined the wolf in enough to do this for her. My cock may seriously break off it's so hard, but pleasuring her is a need fueling me like no other.

Her head wobbles in a nod.

Thank the fates.

I drop to my knees beside the bed and lift one of her legs, propping it on my shoulder. With a flat tongue I lap up the mango juice, cleaning it until I get to her natural essence, that tang that makes my blood hum.

This is where I belong.

It's like my entire life, which has been one giant, walking existential crisis, has been solved between her legs. Pleasuring my female is the only thing that matters in the world. I don't give a fuck about the elders, or even mind that they wanted this, they plotted it. They're probably watching it from the window. I only live for those cries of pleasure coming from Sedona's throat, the way her fingers tear at my hair, urging me on. I make my tongue stiff and penetrate her, then move up to her sweet little clit. I suck on it, flick it, swirl my tongue around it. "Like that, beautiful?"

"No," she moans, pulling my mouth back to her clit. I smile against her flesh, returning to my chosen duty.

Sensing her urgency, I give her more, screwing one finger into her pussy. She's tight—unbelievably tight—and she moans on every exhale like she's about to come. I curl my finger to reach her front wall, sweep it around until I find the place where the tissue wrinkles up when I touch it. Her G-spot.

She screams, rubbing her pussy over my face as her muscles clamp down on my finger in a singularly glorious release.

As if to punctuate the end of the show, the lights in the cell abruptly go out.

3

S *edona*

AS IF I wasn't dizzy enough from my orgasm, the fuckers turned the lights out on us. It would be pitch black to a human. Shifters can see in the dark, so I'm not completely blind.

They must have decided it's our official bedtime. I cling to Carlos' head because I need something real and solid to steady myself.

Carlos mutters a curse and eases my leg down from his shoulder. He traces up my thighs with his palms until he reaches my waist. "Okay, *ángel*?"

"Yeah." I sound winded. Well, an orgasm will do that to you.

His palm coasts over the curve of my buttocks ever so lightly, then he gives them a squeeze. "All right," he clears his throat. "I should let you sleep. I'll take the floor."

He stands and my stomach flips at the loss of his warmth. "I don't mind sharing."

"Oh *muñeca.* I would kill to share a bed with you, but it would end with me pounding that sweet pussy of yours until the lights come back on. So no, I'll take the floor."

Lordy, he knows how to talk dirty. His words skitter over my skin, leaving trails of heat everywhere they touch. The room is still spinning from the best cunnilingus of my life.

No wonder he was offended when I suggested we fool around. A man like Carlos gives everything he has in bed and takes everything in return. He's a total alpha. Dominant. Demanding. I had no idea that kind of thing turned me on, but it does.

Even though he said he'd take the floor, he's still standing beside the bed, staring down at me with the look of a starving man. His erection is huge and long, curving up toward his washboard abs.

I lick my lips, the taste of mango still sweet on them. "M-maybe you should take the pressure off. You know, with your hand."

Carlos exhales audibly. As if he'd been waiting for permission, he immediately fists his cock. "Lie back, doll. Show me what I'm not going to have."

He must have a streak of masochism along with that dominant swagger.

But who am I to deny him? He just gave me the best orgasm of my life. I lie back on the bed and cup my own breasts.

He growls and starts pumping his thick cock. "Are you going to let me paint you with my cum, *muñeca*?"

"Yes," I whisper, before I even know how to answer.

"Sweet wolf," he murmurs.

I reach my fingers between my legs and stroke my pussy.

Carlos' growls fill the room. Emboldened, I crawl up, sit on my heels and open my mouth. Carlos slaps the head of his cock against my tongue as he beats off. "*Carajo*, Sedona. That tongue has been my torture."

I wrap my hands around his fist and pull his cock into my mouth, closing my lips around his girth and stroking the underside with my tongue.

"Oh fates," he groans. I suck harder and bob my head forward and back over his length. "Baby, yes. So sweet." He tunnels his fingers into my hair and then closes them, stopping my head with a gentle tug.

"Such a good girl," he croons as he slowly pushes his cock in my mouth. I tense, knowing I can't take his full length. He stops halfway and eases out, then repeats the action. "Mmm, so good." His voice is deep and raspy. "I can't believe you offered up that sexy mouth of yours. I've been wanting to kiss it since the moment I saw you, Sedona. Now I'm fucking it."

My pussy clenches. I want him to fuck me, but I know that's a bad idea. I swirl my tongue around his cock, taking a long pull.

"Enough," he barks. He sounds angry, and his brows are drawn up tight. He pulls my mouth off using my hair and pushes me onto my back. "Touch yourself."

No argument here. My pussy is dying for round two. I cup my mons, pushing the heel of my hand against my clit and undulating my fingers over the rest.

Carlos roars and cum shoots out his cock in ribbons, covering my breasts, my belly, my thighs. He paints me with it, as if it gives him pleasure to see my skin decorated with his seed. I arch on the bed, my breasts thrusting toward the ceiling, knees falling wide. He shoves my hand out of the way and slaps my pussy, short, sharp slaps right over my clit.

I can't comprehend how he knows such a thing will satisfy me, but it does. It's exactly the right intensity, the right speed, the right sensation. Lights flash before my eyes as I explode into a second orgasm, writhing in ecstasy and agony on the bed.

"Sedona."

Fates, I love the way he says my name.

He falls down on top of me, pinning my wrists, exactly the way I'd imagined, and buries his face in my neck. "Beautiful she-wolf. What will I do with you?" He bites my shoulder, suckles my ear lobe.

Keep me forever.

But that's ridiculous. Just because a wolf gives a good orgasm doesn't mean he's my mate.

No, he can't help himself because we're locked naked in a cell together over the full moon. And lord knows, by the time we get out, I won't ever want to see him again, anyway.

Yeah, that's a lie, but I don't want to examine my feelings on the subject. Not now, anyway.

I close my eyes and breathe in Carlos' scent. It's like the outdoors—woodsy and clean. And delicious.

Carlos releases my wrists and settles beside me on the bed. I roll into him, accept his arm as my pillow. My nose rubs against the smooth skin of his chest. My wolf relaxes. In her opinion, I'm totally safe with him.

I don't know how we got from fucked-up kidnapping situation to this, but I'm going to enjoy it while I can.

~.~

Carlos

Sedona falls asleep in my arms and it's impossible for me to rest. Her scent is up in my nostrils, her bare skin touching mine. I'm hard again in minutes. I close my eyes and distract myself by brooding over the elders. I've been blind to the problems I've seen since I returned to Monte Lobo this month. Things seemed bad, but I didn't want to think the worst of the council. These men stepped in as role models for me when my father died. They supported my education, encouraged me to spread my wings. Or so I thought.

At the time, I'd been grateful to leave. My mother was going mad from my father's death and I was too young to take the role of alpha. The elders stepped up to look after her, and I was relieved not to have to see her suffer day in and day out.

Now I see they were getting me out of their way. I didn't realize just how power crazy and fucked up they were until they pulled this stunt.

When I came home three weeks ago to take my place as alpha, I'd presented the ideas I worked on while I was getting my MBA. In this pack, the alpha doesn't act alone, he must gain support of *el consejo* first. It's always been that way.

The elders tabled most of my suggestions. They had a million reasons why each of my changes wouldn't work. They urged me to go back out in the world and bring back a mate. Let them take care of business here as usual. As they had for years.

I've been frustrated, but I thought I just needed a little more time to prove myself as alpha. I told myself they were reasonable and intelligent men who wanted the best for the pack. But I ignored my gut, which told me *el consejo* had let power cloud their vision.

This stunt proves it. Purchasing a kidnapped American female and holding her prisoner? Are they insane? She has family who will surely seek revenge, and this pack is ill-prepared for war.

And now I know what they think of me as their leader. I'm nothing more than a virile young stud to repopulate the Montelobo bloodline. A puppet or figurehead for the peasants to follow while they make decisions that profit only them.

I've been a goddamn fool. I stayed blind to this situation because I preferred not to see it. Just like I preferred not to return. Since my father's death and my mother's mental illness, the atmosphere at the hacienda has become oppressive, but I chose not to figure out why and fix it. I've failed my pack, and now Sedona is caught in the middle of a horrific power play.

Sedona sighs and rubs her nose in my chest hairs. My cock stretches even longer.

Maybe I should jack off again. Oh fates, now the image of spilling my essence over her gorgeous breasts careens into my mind and it's all over. Before I know it, Sedona's pinned beneath me, my cock straining in the notch between her legs. Her pussy moistens against my thick member, her ass presses against my loins, soft and inviting.

"What the—?"

The urge to penetrate her tight pussy and satisfy my wolf is so great, I can barely reason. *Off. Get off her. Now.*

I throw myself to the side, panting as if I've run a mile. "Lock me up," I rasp. "Put the cuffs on me, doll, or your innocence won't survive the night." I stretch my arm out and lock one wrist in the cuff, then reach the second toward the other cuff. "Do it," I bite out.

Her hands tremble as it snaps in place, which fucking slays me.

"I'm sorry. I'm sorry, Sedona. I didn't mean to." *Madre de Dios*, I almost claimed the girl.

"It's okay." Her voice is shaky. She's on her knees, her glorious hair falling down across her breasts. She stares down at me. "What makes you think I'm innocent?"

"You said you hadn't been with a wolf."

"I'm not prude. And I hate the word *innocent*."

I stretch out my palms where they are cuffed. "Sorry." I can't decide if this is just the alpha female thing of not wanting to admit any weakness, or if she really is a virgin.

She flicks my ear with her finger. "I don't have a lot of experience. That doesn't mean I don't like sex."

Oh fates. Did she have to say that? I suddenly want to find out every single thing she likes about it. But anything I do to her in this cell would be akin to rape. She's here against her will. Thank the fates I'm cuffed and she's safe from me.

Sedona moistens her lips with her tongue and my hips snap in response. She catches the movement, but rather than frightening her, it makes her smile. "Hmm, I thought we took care of this." She grips the base of my cock and gives it a shake.

I groan. "Sit on my face," I plead. I need to satisfy her again, need to taste her nectar.

"I don't know," she says in a teasing voice. "I'm not sure you deserve this pussy after the way you just tried to attack me."

Oh fates. If she goes domme on me, I'm going to smack her ass red when I get out of these cuffs.

And *that* thought does nothing to ease my throbbing member. How I'd love to have this she-wolf face down over my lap, squirming while I deliver a little pain-pleasure. A correction for taking the lead when it belongs to me.

"Baby, you'd better not be keeping that pussy from me. I need to taste it. Now, *muñeca.*"

Sedona's lips curve and her eyelids droop. She crawls up and straddles my face. "This pussy?"

I flick her clit with my tongue. "This pussy." It's torture not being able to use my hands, because I want to grip that lush ass of hers and pull her hips down at the perfect angle, but I have to settle with angling my head. I have her at my mercy for a moment, but she pulls her hips up, dancing away when it becomes too intense. She gets to set the pace, which drives me fucking insane.

"Get that pussy back down on me," I growl, infusing dark authority into my voice.

Her arousal floods her folds as she obeys, and I lap it up, teasing her entrance with my tongue, swirling over her clit.

She grips my cock again and I shudder, nearly coming from the sensation. "I guess I'm supposed to reciprocate."

"No, beautiful. This is for you."

She ignores me and leans down, putting her mouth over my cock.

I shout and flick my tongue over her clit like my life depends on it. She slides her hot wet mouth down, lower and lower, slowing when she reaches the back of her throat, then going on.

"*Carajo... carajo. Muñeca,* tell me you never deep throated those human boys of yours."

"You like that?" she purrs, but lifts her hips from my mouth and crawls away from me.

"What are you doing? Get back here," I demand.

She settles between my legs and smiles. "I'm not sure you're in any position to give orders around here, *señor*."

I yank at the chains holding my wrists and she laughs. "Sedona, there are consequences for she-wolves who tease."

Her smile grows broader. "Oh yeah?" She drops her head to take my cock between her lips again and I close my eyes, the sensation too pleasurable to withstand. She continues her tease, practicing her deep throat skills at her own pace, sometimes pulling off and gagging, but then going right back to it.

My canines lengthen, wolf ready to mark her. I close my mouth and turn my face away, not wanting her to see and be frightened. Not that my Sedona shows fear of much. Considering she's been kidnapped and held prisoner for days now, her resilience is stunning. Growls reverberate in my throat and I can't stop myself from jacking my hips up, thrusting into her mouth.

"Uh-uh." She pulls off entirely and blows on my wet cock. "Who's running this show?"

I thrash my head from side to side. If I try to speak, it'll come out a snarl.

"Do you need some time to cool off?"

"No," I grit through clenched teeth.

She laughs, thoroughly enjoying my misery, and puts her mouth back over my cock. The contrast of the cool air and now her moist heat sends me into a paroxysm of pleasure. I snarl, thrusting up into her mouth without control as cum shoots up my shaft.

"I'm coming," I warn and she pops off, angling my cock so my essence paints her beautiful breasts for the second time tonight.

She uses my cock to smear it over them, then squeezes it

between her breasts, letting me fuck them a few times before she releases my dick with a self-satisfied smirk.

"*Ángel*, I will punish you for that," I growl.

She grins. "You're assuming I'm going to let you out of those cuffs."

I close my eyes with exasperation, but a smile plays on my lips. The lightness in my chest—in my being—is one I've never experienced. My whole life has been darkness. Even my time away from this place, was a time for serious study, dedication, hard work, and achievement. And I always carried the burden of Montelobo. But now, in this moment, with Sedona's teasing smile, I swear I could float off the bed.

But she's not mine to keep, and if I wish to be a mate worthy of her, I need to figure out how to get her free before she's dragged down alongside me.

~.~

COUNCIL ELDER

IT's late but I stand with the four other members of our council outside the prison cell door. None of us will sleep this night. If Carlos doesn't claim the American she-wolf under the influence of the full moon, their communion will be far harder to ensure.

They're close—so playful, but we hadn't counted on his using the shackles on himself.

"Maybe we should turn the lights back on, to make sure they don't sleep," Jose suggests. He'd ordered them to be shut off an hour ago thinking it would free them from any repression. While receptive, the she-wolf appeared to be inexperienced. She does not seem so now, though.

"Food," I suggest. "Let's send in food. And wine." Perhaps Carlos will ask for his shackles to be removed to eat. A plate has already been prepared in expectation that Carlos would demand more to eat, so I pick it up. "Juanito, push this through the serving door."

The boy complies. I pour wine in a plastic tumbler. We would use something more romantic, but we can't risk either of them using anything as a weapon against each other or us, so light plastic is the best we can do.

The she-wolf approaches to investigate. She's spectacular. Judging by the way our small group of elderly males tightens around the door, I'm not the only one who finds his libido has returned when faced with such a symbol of shifter fertility. She's truly a prize. If I weren't so old, I'd claim her as my own. Fight every member of the council to do it, too. That's what concerns me. If she inspires Carlos too much, when we release him, he will be out for blood.

~.~

SEDONA

I NEVER REALLY GOT THE whole horny during the full moon thing before, but I'm crazy turned on right now. I thought only male shifters were affected. And yes, Carlos is definitely having a hard time keeping his wolf in check. I can see it shining in his eyes. The deep chocolate brown flickers with amber lights.

"Is your wolf all black?" I couldn't tell before, he was tearing around the room too fast.

"Yes. Come here," Carlos rumbles and wraps his legs around my waist, dragging me down to his body.

I dance away from him, slipping out from his leg hold with a giggle. Lordy, I want to tussle. My wolf is coming out, too, and I need to run and be chased, to be taken to the ground and held down for my claiming.

Carlos growls his disapproval. "Get over here." I love his bossy tone. It's pure alpha command. On my father or brother, it's annoying. On him, it's ultra-sexy.

I slither close, and lick a line up his six-pack abs.

A rumble of frustration sounds in his throat. "What color is your wolf, Sedona?"

"White."

"*Claro que si.*"

I roll my eyes. "Why *of course*?"

"You really are an angel. White and pure. Nothing like me. Such lightness doesn't belong with dark."

"Carlos..." I sense the weight of all that rides on his shoulders and once more I'm angry on his behalf. I run my nails over his sculpted chest. "You don't have to be dark."

"No?" There's doubt tinging the word. "I'm not sure I've ever known anything different."

I pinch one of his nipples and he growls. "Well, you're a smart wolf. I'm sure you could learn."

His smile is sad, but his gaze is warm, as if I'm a kid who just said something sweet but impossibly naive, like I want to give my bubble gum to the starving kids in Africa.

"What? Why not?" I press.

"I wish you could show me," he says it wistfully, like he knows he can't keep me.

For a moment I can't breathe—his words strangle me. He's right—I'm not sticking around. His problems aren't mine. Except there's a sharp sliver of panic running from my belly button to my solar plexus that says I don't want to leave this wolf.

"You don't need me." I force the words out past the band around my throat. "You have an MBA from Harvard. I'll bet you have all kinds of ideas of how to modernize this place." My words fall flat because I know lightness and dark is so much more than modernization. It's the soul of the place, the mental state of the occupants. Something's made Carlos believe he can't change things. "Tell you what. You get me out of here and... I'll write you." Another crazy twinge in my belly at the thought of being separated.

"You'll send me your fairies, Sedona?"

"Yes. Just promise you won't show them to anyone."

"It will be my secret, though I'm sure I'll want to show your talent to everyone I meet."

My cheeks warm. He knows just how to charm me.

"If I honor your request, there is something you must promise me—"

A scraping sound by the door brings my head up with a snap. A plastic plate of food appears through the little service window at the base of the door, along with a new plastic tumbler. Prison rations. Carlos uses the chains on his wrists to leverage himself to sitting, his brows puckered.

I get up and pad over to retrieve the goods. The cup holds red wine. The plate has an array of cut fruits, crackers, cheese, and chocolate. There's even a mashed avocado with pistachio nuts and a white crumbly cheese. Suddenly famished, I dip a cracker into it and take a bite.

"Dinner is served." I walk back, food and wine in hand. "See? The hospitality here isn't so bad."

He mutters something in Spanish.

"Looks like I get to feed you this time." Proffering the wine, I scoot closer to him on the bed.

"Uh-uh. *No*. Unlock me now."

It's hilarious how firm Carlos is. He'll stand me giving him a blowjob, but apparently feeding him crosses a line.

"Sorry, Charlie." My nipples harden as I hold a cracker with avocado dip up to his lips. There's something hot about serving an alpha wolf in my birthday suit.

He takes a bite, his dark-lashed brown eyes locked on my face. "I should be feeding you," he complains, although his jutting erection proves this is hot to him, too.

I roll my eyes. "You're so old-fashioned."

He arches a brow. "Look where I grew up."

I pop another bite of cracker with dip in his mouth, watch his full lips as he chews.

I kneel beside him, loving the way his eyes rake over my breasts, the hunger there. "Tell me about this place. What's it like? How did you become alpha?"

Clouds storm over his expression. "It's... terrible," he admits. "Completely isolated from the modern world. Not poor, but backwards. We have gold and silver mines, which is part of why the ancestors isolated—to keep them a secret—but the methods of mining are ancient and unsafe. Most of the pack survives on subsistence farming and low wages from the mine. We also have plots of sugarcane, a little coffee, and cacao. All the profits go to my family and the council, who live in this *gran hacienda*."

"The pack is led by the council, not you?"

"Yes, exactly so. I don't know how it came about, but

there has always been a council that makes final decisions for the pack. The alpha is more of a figurehead."

"Well I think your council sucks."

"Indeed." His voice is dark. I feed him a slice of an orange star-shaped fruit.

"Why did you come back?" I think I know. He's a natural alpha, which means he wouldn't shirk responsibility, especially for the weak who might depend on him. But I want to hear what he says.

"You know,"—he gives a humorless chuckle—"if it weren't for my mother I might not have. And sometimes I'm not even sure she knows I'm here."

I wait for the story.

"She suffers from dementia. She has since my father's death. The poor woman doesn't belong here. She was given as a gift to my father from a pack on the coast and although she loved my father, she never took to Monte Lobo."

"Given as a *gift*?"

Carlos nods.

"As in, forced to marry, like some medieval princess? What is this, the Dark Ages?" And I thought my dad's dating policy was old fashioned.

"It may as well be. Monte Lobo is a fortress against time, as well as humans. Most of the pack live as serfs."

"Let me guess. The council keeps it that way." I run my hand through my hair. "This place is messed up. No wonder these assholes think they can just grab me from a beach and present me to their alpha."

Carlos winces. "I know it sounds barbaric to you." His expression turns brooding. "I would never bury a woman in a life she hated."

I can't tell if he's talking about what his father did, or making a promise to me, but a chill runs across my skin.

I take a deep drink from the cup of wine. I'm not a huge drinker, but my brother does run a nightclub. The wine is expensive. Delicious. It warms my entire body. I swallow more and bring it to Carlos' lips.

"What did you want me to promise you?"

He takes a sip and a drip falls down his chin.

I lick it off, laughing when his cock bobs in response. "In exchange for my fairies," I remind him, my voice pure seduction.

"I don't wish this event to traumatize you. You're an extraordinary wolf. You have much to enjoy of life, and much to give."

"Thanks."

"Promise me, when you are free, you will not fear. You will still make your choices. Travel, like you wanted to. Forget this time. Forget me."

"I promise I will live without fear," I whisper. "But, I can never forget." Not this time. Not him. Deep down, I know it's true. I've known him only a few hours, but, somehow, he's a part of me.

"Come here." He lifts his chin, gaze on my lips.

I know he wants a kiss, but I can't resist the temptation to straddle his lap first, then slant my lips over his.

He growls, drawing my lower lip into his mouth, taking control back, even with his wrists bound. He tastes of wine and fruit. His facial hair rubs against my face as he tilts his head and masters me with his kiss, tongue sweeping between my lips.

My breath comes faster, liquid heat pooling between my legs. I moan and rub my clit over his erect cock. His tongue twines with mine. I wonder if these are the kinds of kisses he gives on dates and I'm immediately furious with every girl he's had sex with. As if one of them were here now, waiting to take him away from me, I loop an arm around his neck and claim his mouth right back, pressing my breasts against his muscled chest.

Nothing's ever felt so right in my life. Would it be the worst thing in the world to have sex with him? He's an alpha wolf, a magnificent lover. For a first, it probably doesn't get any better than that. And he doesn't harbor any illusion of keeping me. He just said goodbye, for fates' sake.

The wine is working its magic, along with Carlos' tongue, slipping in and out of my mouth on the same rhythm I'm grinding over his cock.

A wanton sound leaves my mouth. I want him. My wolf wants him.

I look down at his cock erect between us. I shift back and grip it and Carlos breaks off the kiss. I watch him struggle with his wolf, eyes changing from chocolate brown to amber and back to brown.

"Don't do it," he growls.

I freeze. I expected encouragement. Well, he just told me to make my own choices. I line his cock up with my entrance and rub the head in my juices.

His eyes widen, almost with panic. *"Sedona."*

"What?"

"What are you doing, *ángel?*"

I thrust my hips forward and take a half inch of his head into my channel. He's huge and I'm tight, so there's a momentary stretch.

Carlos yanks on the restraints like he wants to stop me.

"Please," I whine. "I need this."

"Sedona, you're killing me."

I wrench back, sitting on my heels. His huge cock waves in front of me, inviting my touch. I wrap my hand around it and he groans.

"I want you." I look him in the eye as I tell him. "I want this."

"You don't know what you're doing." Sweat beads on his forehead, his breath is harsh and labored.

"I do. You told me yourself. It's time I start living my own life. Making my own choices. I choose you." I lean into him. "This is happening."

He shuts his eyes.

I pick up the key to the cuffs. I may have decided to get my V-card punched, but it will probably be a way better experience if he's free, since he's the one who knows what he's doing.

I start to unlock him, and his eyes snap open.

"*No,*" he roars. There's an urgency to his voice that makes my wolf sit up and listen. I have a biological response to his alpha command. My pussy turns molten, my body goes weak with submission. But that only makes me want this more. "Don't uncuff me. You're not safe."

"I don't want to be safe," I remind him. I'm not teasing, not brave. Not when he pulls alpha on me. But I've made my decision. I'm not going to let some male authority take away my choices, like I have my whole life.

I get one of his wrists unlocked. The minute his hand comes free, he snatches my nape and yanks my mouth to his. His tongue plunges before I can catch my breath. He dominates my mouth, punishing me with a hard, demanding kiss.

But when he breaks away, he shakes his head, his dark eyes glowing amber at the edges. "I can't," he pants, "—not safe."

But my wolf needs this as much as his. She's decided she's having him. My fingers tremble as I release the second wrist cuff.

Carlos is free.

He lunges for me. In a flash, I'm flat on my back knees spread up to my shoulders. Carlos attacks my pussy with his mouth, hungry, devouring. He sucks and nips my labia, suctions his mouth right over my clit and pulls hard.

I scream, back bowing up on the mattress.

Fates, yes.

"*Fuck, Sedona,*" he growls, palming my ass, squeezing my cheeks firmly enough to leave marks. It satisfies me on a deep level, his intensity meets the burning need within me.

He drags his open mouth up my belly and latches his lips over my nipple, biting before sucking it hard.

I arch up, pussy contracting as I feel the ghost of his tongue still there. "Please," I whimper. I don't need foreplay. In fact, I'll die if he gets me any more aroused. I need satisfaction. No tongue. No fingers. Even though I've never had a cock, my instincts scream for consummation in that way. I somehow know nothing else will do but to feel the hard length of him moving between my legs.

Carlos pops off my nipple and shocks me to my toes by slapping the same breast he'd just pleasured.

"*Oh.*" I didn't even know that was a thing, but I freaking love it. "Carlos, please. I'm ready."

He slaps my breast again. His brows are drawn low; passion, hunger, pure animal nature burns in his eyes. Anger, too, because he's still working hard to keep his wolf in check. "You'll take whatever I give you, *muñeca*. I *told* you *not* to unlock me. In fact, I think a little punishment is in order."

Wait... what? I jerk up onto my elbows.

He scoops me into his arms, spins around and sits on the side of the bed, draping me over his lap. His hand crashes down three times before I can wiggle my ass. "That's for teasing me, *mi amor*."

Oh, it's on. My wolf wants to struggle, only to feel his mastery. If we were in animal form, he'd be chasing me through the woods now, nipping my flank.

He keeps spanking. "And this is for not listening. The cuffs were for *your safety*."

Oh lordy. My ass burns, but it feels so right. Again, it's exactly the intensity I crave. I need this pain, need something to ease the pressure building inside me.

Because my wolf craves the game, I kick and try to throw myself off him, but he's quick, clamping his leg over mine and pinning my wrists behind my back. I love feeling his physical power, how easily he holds me in place for his punishment. He keeps slapping my ass. The heat his spanks produces is wonderful. Intoxicating.

"You over-estimate my control, *muñeca*. You think I can give you what you desire without tearing you up?"

Tearing me up sounds a little scary, but I do still have faith in him. He won't lose control. Not when he cares this much about keeping me safe.

"Fates. *This ass*." I'm guessing that's a compliment. The rich baritone of his voice reverberates in my lady parts. He slaps one of my cheeks and then the other. "It was *made* for spanking."

I shiver, the idea of real discipline at his hands making something strange slither in my belly. Wolves are, by nature, ruled by physical dominance. Swift corporal correction comes within the pack, and also between partners. Wolves heal quickly, so there's no harm, no foul to any of it. It's dominance played out, re-establishing who's on top. I've never been afraid of it, but I never knew it would be this exciting. Sexual. Pleasurable. Or maybe it's just this way with Carlos. Or during the full moon.

But no, I know the thrumming need between my thighs has nothing to do with the full moon and everything to do with being mastered by this sexy wolf, having my ass painted red by his large, powerful hand.

I squeeze my thighs together, trying to ease the throb in my swollen sex. Carlos spanks me with a steady beat. As the pain begins to set in, I squeeze my bottom and writhe over his lap, trying to dodge the slaps. "Carlos," I gasp. My ass tingles and burns.

"Sedona." His deep voice is still rough. He catches the back of my thigh, where the flesh is more tender.

"Oh!"

His erection juts into my hip, torturing me with its closeness, as I tortured him earlier.

"Please," I plead.

His spanking hand fists my hair and he pulls my head up. "You think I have *any* control when you're wiggling this juicy ass all over my lap?"

"More," I gasp hoarsely.

He growls, a rich sound that rumbles in his chest and sends my toes curling. When he starts to spank again, the slaps fall even harder, but my flesh, already warm and tingling, seems to welcome the blows. I still squirm under the onslaught, my better instincts trying to avoid the pain, even as my baser ones welcome it.

"Carlos." Need threads my voice.

"That's right, beautiful. Say my name." He catches the back of my other thigh, making me cry out. "Say it again."

"Carlos!"

He picks up both the speed and intensity of his slaps, so

the blows fall one after the next, stinging and smarting every inch of my bottom.

"Ouch, Carlos! Ow, please! Oh... oh!" It's too much and not enough all at once. I lift my bottom to greet his hand, part my thighs, moisture dripping from my wanton pussy.

"Please what?" He's panting as hard as I am.

I kick my feet and hump his lap, wild for something more, something less, for everything.

He pauses, then gives me one more hard slap and pulls me up to sit on his lap, facing away from him. He parts his knees, dragging my legs, which were tangled over the tops of his, wide. "You still want more, Sedona?" His breath is scorching hot on my ear. "You're going to get this pussy spanked." He wraps a firm arm around my waist and brings his hand down between my legs.

"Ooh, ooh!" I squeal, but leave my knees open.

He slaps again. With his other hand, he crushes my breast, massaging too hard. After the third spank against my dripping folds, I practically sob with need. Thankfully, his fingers stay and cup my mons. I squirm against them. He screws one finger in and I grab his hand and urge it deeper. "So wet for me." He groans, like a broken man. "Impossible to resist."

I struggle, need making me impatient. The struggle satisfies everything, though. I manage to squirm out of his grip and he tackles me onto the bed, catching my wrists and pinioning them in one hand over my head.

He rises up over me. Dark determination wrestles with wild wolf in his expression.

I spread my legs, curl my pelvis up for him as his hips settle over mine. He brings one hand down to grip his cock, pain rippling over his face like he's fighting for control.

"Yes, *yes*, Carlos." I'm moaning like a porn star and he hasn't even penetrated me.

He rubs his cock over my slit and I moan louder.

This velvet soft flesh over rock-hard muscle is precisely what I've missed my whole life. Fingers are a poor substitute. "Give it to me."

In a single thrust, he fills me and I scream in shock. His cock is so much bigger than his finger. I feel the head hit deep inside while he stretches my entrance wide.

"Sedona!" His eyes fly wide, only frenzied breaths issue from his frozen form. *"Ángel, no."*

I guess it's obvious I was a virgin. I don't know why I didn't want to admit it earlier.

His gaze glows pure amber now, sweat drips down his temples, but somehow he keeps from moving his hips. He's a goddamn saint for holding back. I may have begged for it, but I struggle to catch my breath from the burst of pain when he plowed me open.

"You should have told me," he growls over clenched teeth. "You deserve so much better than this."

He may regret popping my cherry, but I'm not sorry. Already, the sharp pain is gone and the sensation of being filled by him is pure heaven. My hips move of their own accord. "Shut up." I thrust them upward. "Give it to me, Carlos."

Carlos shudders, eyes back to brown—no, black. With his face screwed up in pained concentration, he rocks his hips.

It's a mixture of pain and pleasure for me, then the pain recedes and pleasure floods every cell in my body. "More." I wrap my legs around his waist and urge him deeper, faster.

Carlos roars and slams into me, animal unleashed. His

eyes flash amber as he fists the chains on the bedposts and fills me over and over again.

I throw my hands up to the wall to keep my head from hitting. He pulls out and gives his head a shake. I think he's trying to speak but all that comes out are growls. He rises up on his knees, cupping my ass, which he lifts in the air with him. He holds me at an angle, pulls my hips to meet his thrusts, getting so deep inside I swear he'll split me open.

My eyes roll back in my head, mouth open for my steady cries.

Carlos fills the room with growls, amber eyes fire-like against the dark of his hair and skin. I wonder if mine have changed to ice-blue. Just as I'm about to come, he pulls out, flips me over and pulls my hips up so I'm on my knees. When I climb to my hands, he shoves between my shoulder blades, forcing my upper body down.

Oh. Apparently he likes the angle thing.

As soon as he enters me, I understand why. Fates, he's even deeper from this position, but it feels so right. He grips my hips with bruising force and plows into me, his loins slapping hard against my still smarting ass, cock gliding in and out at the perfect trajectory. His balls slap my clit.

It's hard to imagine being fucked any harder than this, but there's no pain, no discomfort, no fear. I'm drowning in pleasure and only Carlos knows how to give it to me. I quite possibly lose my mind, maybe I black out, maybe I shot to Jupiter for a moment. The next thing I know, Carlos' snarls roar in my ear. I'm coming, my muscles gripping his cock and squeeze-releasing over and over again. He drags us both down flat, me on my belly, his body covering mine.

And then he bites me.

~.~

SEDONA'S YELP of pain brings me back from the brink and I realize my teeth are buried in her shoulder. *Mierda.*

I disengage my fangs and lap her wound, licking away the blood, providing the healing enzymes of my saliva for her quick recovery. It's not the actual wound that's the problem, though. It's the ramifications of what I've done.

Marked her.

She'll carry my scent for the rest of her life. More than that, I'm bonded forever to her. As much as I may have wanted to fight the elders to set her free, I will now kill anyone who tries to take her from me.

Fuck.

"I'm sorry," I rasp. I ease my cock from her glorious channel and roll off her. I mean to scoop her into my arms, but she shifts, whether out of fury or pain, I don't know. "Sedona."

Her wolf is gorgeous—snow white with silver tipped ears and the palest of blue eyes. Big, healthy. Beautiful. She stalks around the room, moving stiffly like I've caused her pain in more places than her shoulder.

Double fuck. I'm the king asshole of the continent.

"I'm sorry. I didn't mean to mark you, *ángel.*" I can't stand to see her pace this way—my need to comfort her is too great, and it's harder in wolf form. I stand from the bed, and meet her in the center of the room. She swings her head to turn from me. "Sedona, *shift.*" I infuse every bit of alpha command into my voice. She will be unable to disobey, even though it will make her angry.

She shifts, unfolding from a crouched position, fury blaring from her eyes. She walks forward and slaps me across the face.

I take it. I deserve this. I deserve much worse. I have forever bound her to me after promising to help her get free. "Forgive me. Please."

Tears swim in her eyes. "What you did can't be undone, Carlos."

I bow my head. "I know."

"What do you know?" she demands.

I know this conversation isn't going to be productive, but I also know she's pissed off and needs a way to let it out. I know I want to hold her, to comfort her, but I'm loathe to force my comfort on her if she hates me now.

I turn away from her, frustrated. Fury at *el consejo* returns. I pick up the iron bed and throw it against the wall where it clatters and falls to its side.

Sedona's eyes round.

Because there's nothing else to do, I pick it up and throw it again, this time in the direction of the door. I know these room are made of steel, that I won't beat my way out, even with an iron bed, but I'm not above trying.

When I pick it up a third time, Sedona shouts, "Stop!" I turn to find her holding her hands over her ears, tears swimming in those beautiful blue eyes.

I storm her, picking her up against my body with an arm around her waist and walking until her back hits the wall. I kiss her, sucking her lips, claiming her mouth with the ownership of a mate. It's not fair. It's not right. But she's mine now. There's nothing I can do to change that.

My thigh presses between her legs and I don't stop

tormenting her mouth, fucking it with my tongue, mopping it with my lips. I taste her tears and it only fuels this need to consume her, to devour her. To further establish my claim on her because my wolf knows she's already slipped away.

"Sedona." I pull back, let her see every ounce of misery in my being. "I won't apologize again." I pound the wall beside her head with my fist. "I'm *not* sorry. *Not* sorry for claiming you."

She sucks in her breath, staring at me with wide eyes.

"You are the prize above all other prizes, and I got to you first," I say through gritted teeth. It's wrong, but what I'm saying feels so right. Passion blazes bright in my chest, flowing down my limbs. "You belong to me. I've taken you. I will never let you go. And I'm not sorry. You are perfect in every way. Smart, talented, beautiful." I manage to pry my fist open to touch her cheek. "Funny. You are the light to my darkness. You brought me to life. All these years, I've been half-dead. It was the only way to survive the pain of my mother's illness, my father's death. The heaviness that belongs to my pack. But you—you sparked me back to life. And for that I cannot be sorry. I *cannot*. So I beg your forgiveness. I do. But I could never regret claiming you. Not in this lifetime, or any other."

Sedona's lips tremble. I have no idea what she's thinking, what she's feeling. Whether she's scared of me or wants to cut my balls off. I didn't lie. I told her the goddamn truth, and if that makes her hate me forever, so be it. At least she knows.

If I weren't so out of my mind, I would have registered the sound behind me sooner. The door opens. Sedona jerks in fear and a sharp stab lands between my shoulder blades. The last thing I see is a dart land in my female's chest before we both crumple to the floor.

4

C*arlos*

I WAKE IN MY BEDROOM. The scent of Sedona is still in my nostrils and I reach for her, but my arms come up empty. The memory of seeing her last returns and I bolt upright with a gasp.

Sedona. Where is my female? The urgency to find her, protect her, nearly makes me shift. If those motherfuckers laid one finger on my female, I will rip them to shreds. I don't care if I'm banished forever from this pack. Even if it means leaving my poor mother. I will not stand by and let my female be mistreated.

I surge from the bed and throw on a pair of pajama pants before pounding toward the door. A light but rapid tap sounds on it. The door pushes open before I can say *pásale.*

Juanito bursts in. "Don Carlos, It's your mother. She's having a fit. Come quickly."

Screams reach my ears.

"*Déjame!*" my mother's raw voice echoes in the center courtyard. *Leave me.* Sedona's fading scent clings to me as I run out and look down into my mother's garden, the center courtyard the hacienda is built around. Mamá paces alone, her skirts aflutter. The servants huddle at the edges of the garden. She turns in a circle, long grey hair flying. Sweat drips down her face, her eyes are wild.

"*Mamá!*" I run for the marble stairs and take them two at a time.

My mother doesn't seem to even hear me. She's babbling something, as if arguing with demons or ghosts. She tears at her nightdress. "*Déjame sola!*"

"Mamá!" I reach her and grip her arms, trying to get her wild focus to settle on my face. I don't succeed. She pulls to get away from me. Tears streak her face, once lovely, now sallow with dark circles under her eyes.

I could overpower her, of course, but I can't bring myself to manhandle my mother. "Mamá, it's all a dream. None of it is real. Look at me. Your son. Look at Carlos."

"Carlos?" Her voice rings with panic. "Where's Carlitos? What have they done with my little boy? They want to kill him, too."

"No, Mamá, I'm right here—Carlos—Carlitos—all grown up. Look at me."

Her unsteady gaze wavers around the courtyard and skips around my face. She reaches out to touch it, her brow wrinkling. "Carlos?"

"*Si,* Mamá, I'm right here."

She grabs my hand and tries to pull me further into the

center of the garden. "Hurry, Carlos. We have to run. Before they get you, too. Every alpha is in danger."

I don't move, forcing her to shift her grip to two hands and tug with all her might. "No, I'm not in danger. I can defend myself. And you. We're safe, I promise. Come—this way." I wrap my palm around hers. "Let's go to your room."

Her eyes widen. "My prison, you mean?" She shakes her head wildly. "That's where they want to keep me quiet. I don't want to go there. I want to leave, Carlos. Take me away from this place."

Pain rips through my chest. Should I find a way to send her back to her own pack? She still hates it here after all these years. But would they even take her? A crazy woman who requires full-time care? Would they provide the level of treatment she requires? I've never met anyone from Mamá's old pack, or any pack other than my own. I feel the wrongness of that deep into my bones. I should've done it when my father died. Not ten years later. My head aches with the weight of my guilt, my responsibility.

"Okay, I'll take you away from here," I promise, praying I can keep my word. "But I need time to figure out where and how. So let's get you back to your bedroom—"

"Not my bedroom!" she shrieks. "Not there! Don't take me there, Carlos." She's suddenly weeping, like she's the child and I'm the parent.

I pull her against my chest and stroke her tangled hair. "Okay, not your bedroom," I agree. I look around desperately, trying to figure out what else to do with her. "How about a walk in the outer garden with Maria Jose?" I make eye contact with Juanito's mother, Mamá's servant, and nod.

Maria Jose approaches slowly.

My mother sniffs and pulls away, nodding. *"Sí."*

My shoulders sag. I tug her hand in Maria Jose's direction. "Maria will keep you safe, Mamá. I'll see you after your walk, all right? I'll see you for breakfast."

After I find Sedona.

My mother toddles away on Maria Jose's arm, but Juanito scuttles over to me. "Don Carlos," he says in a low, urgent tone. He looks around like he's afraid of being seen, and I have no doubt someone is watching, somewhere.

I grip his arm and tug him into the shadows. *"Qué cosa?"*

"The Americans are here to rescue your female. *El consejo—*"

The bell in the bell tower starts to toll, signaling the pack of danger. Don Santiago enters. Something about the timing of his appearance seems deliberate. "There you are." His voice is smooth as caramel. "We have a problem. Three large vans breached the outer gate. Prepare to fight for your female."

Ice flushes through my veins as I see their plan. They're banking on my strength to fend off these enemies they brought onto our pack. My mind races. I don't even know where my female is, and I'm sure as hell not going to fight her family for her. That will not inure the beautiful American to me. With a calmness I don't feel, I squeeze Juanito's shoulder. "Run and grab me a shirt, Juanito. I'll be right behind you." I turn to Jose. "Gather the males of the pack and tell them to meet on the terrace." I infuse alpha authority into my voice, even though I know full well my orders mean nothing to this man. The council has been running me now for years. I run up the stairs and meet Juanito at the top, carrying my shirt. I grab it from him and pull it on as I murmur in a low voice. "Where is my female, Juanito?"

"Locked in a guest room in the east wing, Don Carlos."

"Can you find a way to set her free?"

"I-I don't know, sir." Juanito is a smart kid, I know he'll figure it out.

"I need you to try. Let her out and take her out to her people through the lower gate. Don't let anyone see you. The future of this pack depends on you, my friend."

Juanito's lowered eyes jerk up to mine and I watch honor fill his being. "Yes, sir." He slips away, quiet and invisible as a ghost.

I head out to the terrace, where the men of our pack are gathering, in from the mines and the fields, watching the white vans wind up the mountain toward the citadel. "We will defend our pack, if necessary, but there will be no violence without a cue from me, understood?" I use every bit of alpha power in my voice, making it boom and project confidence, leadership. The trouble is, these males have never fought with me before, never taken my orders.

Most of them are old. The only younger male shifter in the pack besides myself was Juanito's brother, Mauca, but he disappeared last year. Ran away, is what they said, but I know Juanito and Maria Jose don't believe that. There aren't many other male shifters under the age of fifty, except the *defectuosos*. They are here, though, armed with machetes, ready to fight as men.

Guillermo, the big wolf who runs the mines is here, along with his men. I can count on them to defend the pack, if it comes to that.

Don Santiago and the rest of the council are here, but they are not preparing to fight. No, they are setting up as if to watch a football match. Granted, they are all over seventy, but shifters live long lives and heal quickly. I think they play the privilege card and the elderly card far too often. As I look at their self-satisfied faces, I want to beat the right-eousness out of every one of them.

And what better diversion? Especially with an audience. It's time to establish exactly who is alpha in this pack. A growl rips from my throat as I stalk over. I grab the first one I get to—Don Mateo—and grasp him by the throat. My fingers wrap right around his chicken neck and I lift him from the ground. "*You* brought this attack on our pack," I roar. "You and the rest of the council."

"Put him down," Don Jose snarls. He uses his usual superior command, but it falls flat in the face of alpha rage. He turns to the pack. "The boy has inherited some of his mother's lunacy."

Oh, fuck no. Of course they'd try that tactic. Make me look insane.

I look around at the council. They might treat me like a treasured pup, but these aren't the grandfatherly men who raised me. These are powerful wolves. "You *purchased* a female—an American—stolen from her pack by traffickers. What did you think would happen?"

Don Santiago goes for a smug, unruffled tone. "We thought you would claim her, and we were correct."

Don Mateo's face turns red as he struggles to drag in gurgling breaths. His feet kick out uselessly. The men of the pack move in close, crowding around us, but no one—including the other elders—physically challenges me. Together, they could take me down, but not without a lot of bloodshed.

"You locked me in my own dungeon. Disrespected your alpha. Do you think that deed will go unpunished?"

Mateo's eyes bulge. If I don't release him soon, he'll die.

Out of the corner of my eye, I see Guillermo step forward. The burly wolf isn't high in the pack, but with his miners behind him, they could overpower me. If the council gave the order, I could be dead, and my mother with me. I'm surrounded by the pack I'm supposed to lead, and I don't know who I can trust.

"*Tranquilo*, Carlos. It was not out of disrespect, but out of love. We provided you with a prize worthy of an alpha like you," Don Santiago placates.

I drop Mateo not because I'm playing good little alpha for the council, but as much as I'd like to kill him and all the dons, I'm not a murderer. Whirling to face Don Santiago, I let out a ferocious growl. Every wolf around me drops his eyes and shows his throat in submission.

Better.

"Now you disrespect my female. She is not an object, but an alpha she-wolf, capable of tearing out any one of your throats. If any of you ever touch or confine her against her will again, you're dead. *Comprendes?*"

"*Sí*, Don Carlos." The males of the pack mutter the answer automatically. I'm not sure I hear it from the lips of the elders, but they nod their heads as if in agreement. *Lying fuck-toads.*

This isn't finished. Even though I've heard what I demanded to hear, I'm not even close to satisfied. "I will consider your punishment," I growl.

Yeah, I don't know how that will go down. Will I have the ability to enforce a punishment on council members? I don't have a fucking clue, but I sure as hell know I'm not going to let them off easy in front of my pack.

Behind me, the pack members shift in discomfort. They are either more loyal to, or more afraid of the council. I get that. I've only been back a few weeks. They don't know me, and it will take time for me to prove myself as a leader. But I certainly intend to do that.

"Later." Don Santiago points down at the road outside the walls surrounding our citadel. "The Americans have arrived." The three white vans pull up outside the front portcullis and stop. Their doors open and dozens of muscled wolves pour out, young males in their prime, arms covered in tattoos, weapons in their hands.

~.~

SEDONA

THE BOY who let me out of the bedroom where I was locked beckons me forward. We're outside the palace or castle—or whatever they call this building. It's certainly regal enough to be a castle. In fact, we're heading along the same path the men carried my cage on when I arrived. Above us, looms the gleaming building, below us but still within the walls of the enclave are little huts with thatched roofs.

I woke up alone in a canopied bed dressed in a ridiculous flowing robe, like some medieval princess. Fitting as I was locked in a tower. This place is seriously stuck in the seventeenth century.

I tried the door, but it was locked. Pounding on it got me nowhere. Neither did calling for Carlos, but then the boy showed up, put his finger to his lips to silence me and rushed me out of the building.

Now that we're outside, he speaks to me in Spanish, but I don't have a clue what he's saying.

"Juanito?" I ask. "Are you Juanito?"

He stops and turns, and his serious face splits into a grin. "*Sí, soy Juanito.*" He bobs his head, as if I just did him some great honor by knowing his name. He rattles off something else, but all I catch is "Carlos."

"Where is Carlos?" I ask. I'm more than a little disappointed to be rescued by the boy instead of the male who marked me last night. It's stupid, but I feel abandoned. I need to see him. We need to talk about the fact that he marked me, and what it means.

But I guess escaping the crazy council should be the first order of business. Juanito pulls a keycard from a cord around his neck and flashes it against a surprisingly high-tech lock on a gate in the polished adobe wall.

Outside, I hear... English voices.

I surge forward, running toward the sound, and I recognize males from both my brother and father's packs piling out of three white bus-sized super-vans parked outside a giant portcullis. I have no idea how they found me, but relief nearly drowns me.

My brother senses me coming and whirls. "Sedona?"

I'm sure I look ridiculous in the flowing robe. Tears sting my eyes. I fly at him, wrapping my arms and legs around him. The force of my hug drives my huge big brother to take a step back.

As soon as Garrett's arms close around me, I know everything's going to be all right. He's bigger and stronger than any of the fuckers who took me captive. The only exception might be Carlos, but I can't think about him right now.

"It's okay," Garrett murmurs. I press my face into his shoulder, clutching him. His muscles flex around me, big, protective. "No one's gonna hurt you. Never again."

"Sedona," a deep voice makes me raise my head. My dad stands beside us, lips pressed tight together—a look I'm all too familiar with. For once I'm glad to see it.

"Dad." I turn to him and give him a heartfelt, if stiffer hug. It's only when I draw back and study the deep lines etched on my father's brow that I realize his stern look isn't one of disapproval. It's worry—and now deep relief.

"I'm sorry," my voice cracks.

"It's all right," Garrett soothes, at the same time my father says, "We'll talk about it later."

I lean into my big brother's side, unable to look my father in the eyes. Garrett gives me a squeeze—another signal I'm familiar with from the times I've gotten in trouble. *You and me, sis. Dad's gonna be a hardass, but we'll get through it—together.* Even though he's eight years older, and as alpha and protective as our dad, Garrett has always stuck by me.

I don't think my big brother can fix this. We're in some godforsaken mountain in Mexico, facing off with an unfamiliar pack, deep in hostile territory. My dad might be dealing with the political ramifications of this for the next thirty years.

It's my fault. I'm the alpha's daughter. It's my responsibility to follow the rules—for the good of the pack. Me and my stupid idea to live it up on spring break.

"How do we get in? I'm going to kill every last motherfucking—" Garrett's cracking his knuckles when I cut in.

"*No.*" I still don't know what in the hell is going on here. Carlos must have sent Juanito to set me free. But where is Carlos? I look back where Juanito stands, looking uncertain. Is Carlos coming? He can't. My heart fills with lead. If he did, my father and Garrett would kill him. No, I need to get out of here before any wolves—on either side—get hurt. I couldn't stand having blood on my head. "Take me out of here. I don't want a fight. I just want to go home. Let's go."

My dad shakes his head. "No one steals my daughter and lives."

"They didn't steal me, they bought me. You're welcome to kill the fuckers who stole me, but they're not here. I just want to leave. No bloodshed. Please." I catch Garrett's eye and hold his gaze, silently pleading.

He grabs my dad's arm and they walk around the back of the van to confer in private.

Of course, because I have shifter hearing, I don't miss any of the conversation.

"Dad, don't you think Sedona's been through enough? She's been *mated*."

My eyes fill with tears. Hunching, I cover the already healed wound on my shoulder. In a few days it would be nothing more than a slight scar, but I will carry Carlos' scent, a trace of his essence, with me until I die.

Garrett continues in a low voice, "She might have conflicted feelings toward the guy. The last thing she needs is more trauma. If she says no bloodshed here, I think we have to honor her wishes."

"We don't kill them and we send the message we're weak."

They argue some more, but when they come back around, my father clips, "Everyone back in the vehicles."

Garrett shoos me into his van and climbs in the back seat beside me, throwing his strong arm around my shoulders.

As the van takes off down the mountain, I try to pull it together, but my emotions are all over the place. I hate being the victim, rescued by the males in her family. It's pathetic and I know if I dip into that, even for a second, I could tumble into a pool of self-pity so deep I could let this experience scar me for the rest of my life.

Poor Sedona, they would whisper about me. *She's never been the same since her abduction and rape.*

Fuck that. I was a victim, yes. But it wasn't rape. I begged him for it. And I'm not weak, I'm an alpha female. I can turn this into a win, not a loss.

But what did I win?

I had my V-card punched, in the most incredible, satisfying way. It's hard to imagine it gets much better than what we shared. But I also walked away marked. I'm not even sure of the ramifications of carrying a male's scent when I didn't choose him as a mate.

Carlos let me go.

Fates, thinking of him sends a searing pain right through the middle of my chest. Will I ever see him again? Do I want to? It's a fucked up kind of complicated, isn't it?

I still don't even know if he was as innocent in my imprisonment as he insisted. What if he orchestrated the whole damn thing?

But no, why let me go, then? And I'm sure it was Carlos who sent Juanito to shuttle me out to my family. Whether it was to save his own pack or for my benefit, I can't be sure. Because I know one thing—my family's packs would have *brought it.*

So logically, it seems like I should count Carlos releasing me as a win. Why, then, does it seem like my heart is beating outside my chest? Like it stayed back on that mountain and the further we drive away, the more anxious I become at leaving it behind?

But please. Did I want him to claim me? To keep me?

Fuck no.

I would never stay on that godforsaken mountain with that crazy pack. They're the most backwards, insane bunch I've ever seen, and my father has hosted a lot of pack mingles over the years.

Even if they were the most charming wolves on Earth, I

wouldn't want to stay. I'm twenty-one years old. I haven't even finished college. I only just started having fun. Fates, my spring break vacation in San Carlos seems so long ago. So far away. What did my friends think when I disappeared from the beach?

"How did you find me?" I ask Garrett, speaking for the first time in what must have been a couple hours. I applaud him for not grilling me the whole way, but Garrett is perceptive. I'm glad I didn't ride in my father's van.

"My mate found you."

Wait... what? Garrett doesn't have a mate. He's been playing Mr. Bachelor for years with his pack of young males. "Your *mate*?"

Garrett touches my fresh mark. "Looks like we both mated this moon."

Garrett sounds so happy. I'm going to go out on a limb and guess his mating was nothing like mine. He wasn't locked naked in a room with her and forced to mate. He chose a female. The way I always thought I'd get to choose a mate.

And now I'm wallowing in self-pity—the swamp I didn't want to swim in. "Tell me about her?" I need distraction.

"Her name is Amber. She's a human psychic and an attorney. And my next door neighbor. When you went missing, I volun-told her we needed her help, and we brought her along to Mexico. She helped us follow your trail to Mexico City, where we found your original captors."

I scowl, remembering the cage and the warehouse.

"They're already dead," Garrett assures me.

"A human?" Garrett mated a human? It's unheard of for an alpha wolf to take a human mate. I hope this doesn't mean he'll lose his position as alpha. His pack is as loyal as they come, but you never know. Some wolf may challenge him for it. The most likely contender would be Tank, his beta, except that Tank is from our father's pack originally and his loyalty there would prevent it.

"My wolf picked her." Garrett shrugs but his goofy grin says he's hopelessly in love.

Is that what happened with me and Carlos? Our wolves picked even though our human selves never would have?

What about all that stuff Carlos said just before we were drugged? About not being sorry he'd mated me? Was that the truth? Or just the effect of the full moon and a happy inner wolf?

"You sure you don't want me to go back there and kill the entire Montelobo pack? Because I won't hesitate if you give the word."

"*No.*" I twist and grab Garrett's shoulders before I realize what I'm doing. "You can't do that."

Garrett falls silent, searching my face. My grip tightens. "You can't. Promise me." What if Carlos were hurt? Or someone he cared about, like his mother or Juanito?

"You sure, kiddo?" His voice is mild, but for a second I glimpse the cold-hearted predator lurking behind the human facade. The wolf would kill first and ask questions never, leaving a trail of bodies behind.

"I'm sure. Don't let dad go back, either. Promise me."

"All right, sis. Calm down. I promise." I can tell he wants to ask me more, so I turn in his arms, tucking myself into his side. I hold him tight until my racing heart slows down.

Our van rolls through a sprawling city, which Garrett tells me is the country's capital, Mexico City. We stop at a skyrise hotel and Garrett shifts in his seat, his eyes fixed on a high story window. His mate must be inside.

Ugh. I rub my nose. What would it be like to be happily mated instead of leaving the most fucked up of matings possible? "So where's Amber, now?" I try for enthusiasm. I'm going to have a sister for the first time. With Garrett so much older, I'm more like an only child. "When can I meet her?"

"She's in our suite. Come on. You can meet her now."

Garrett leads me into the hotel and up an elevator, but when he enters his room, I know something's wrong. There's no scent of a female present—human or otherwise.

Garrett picks up a note and reads it, then roars, smashing his fist into a wall.

Well, crap.

I guess I'm not the only one whose mating is a mess.

5

Carlos

I WALK along the outside perimeter of our citadel. The buzzing in my ears makes my head pound, but I keep pushing on. I'm going to walk the entirety of our pack territory every day until I know who lives in which hut, the names of their family members, what they do for us. Even as I vow it, though, the landscape goes by without my seeing a thing.

All I see is Sedona, chained naked to that bed. My terrible, wonderful prize.

Watching her leave was like allowing someone to steal away with a vital organ from my body. I stood there, numb, not understanding how I still lived, still breathed without her here. It took all my willpower not to shift and chase after her pack's vans like a common dog. Not to howl.

But somehow I managed to stay on the terrace and watch, keeping my pack out of danger.

The council couldn't believe I let her go. When they saw her standing out there, her white filmy wrap threading around her legs in the breeze, their pompous airs dropped.

"Why is your female out of her room?" Santiago demanded.

"I set her free," I said calmly.

"Are you mad?" Mateo asked. "She's your mate."

Yes, mine, my wolf howled.

But it doesn't matter. I wasn't going to show my teeth to her pack, to her family. It was wrong to keep her this way. Wrong to have bought her in the first place. Everything we'd done to her had been wrong.

"Go and fight for your female. Or are you too much of a coward?" Don Santiago challenged.

I punched him in the face. I would never do something like that to an elderly human, but an old shifter can take it. The pack surged around me—I didn't know whether they meant to stop me if I continued, but no one touched me.

"Crazy, like his mother," Don Jose proclaimed.

"I'm not keeping a female against her will," I snarled. "Not even one I've marked. And if any of you here believe such a thing is acceptable, you are the reason this pack is falling to ruin." I turned in a circle, meeting every male's eyes, forcing their gaze to drop in the face of my dominance. A small victory, but it satisfied my wolf.

Don Santiago rubbed his jaw and climbed to his feet. "So, what? You're not going to fight to win her love? Her affection? I daresay you already had it."

My heart squeezed painfully, then, and it's still squeezing. I want to believe that much is true. But it could've been simple biology. The council knew exactly what they were doing putting a fertile she-wolf naked in a cell with a virile male over the full moon. And the adversity brought us together. Holding her to anything based on what we shared in there wouldn't be fair. She had no choice but to accept me. It doesn't mean she wants me as her mate. If she did, she wouldn't have been so quick to jump in that van and disappear.

But even if she never wants to see me again, I will still avenge her. I gave the council one week to produce the traffickers who kidnapped her. When they hedged, I made it clear. "I will have blood for what was done to my female. Either it's yours, or theirs."

They'd better deliver.

I walk on the edge of a small coffee grove. The front of Monte Lobo is covered in trees, but small farm plots make up the entire back side of the mountain, forming a patchwork quilt of color and texture. This extinct volcano we call Monte Lobo doesn't provide the best climate for coffee—not like the coastal states like Chiapas—but our pack has always been able to grow enough for our own use. It's actually impressive the variety and quantity of crops our pack produces simply for our own subsistence.

Centuries ago, when our Spanish ancestors settled peacefully with the indigenous people who lived here, they set up a wonderful system for sustainable living in isolation. They frightened the indigenous people off, not through violence, but by inciting their superstitions. Men who change into wolf form at the full moon won the awe and respect of the tribe, which moved to the base of the mountain and guarded it from outside visitors. It allowed our pack to shut themselves away.

"*Buenas tardes*, Don Carlos." An elderly wolf in dirty, worn clothing and a wide-brimmed hat stops what he's doing to greet me. Despite the greeting, he looks wary, or suspicious of me.

I stop and lift my hand in greeting. Judging by the way he scrutinizes me, he already knows what happened today. Or was he there? It's sad that I'm not even sure. I don't even know this wolf's name. I've been a piss-poor leader of this pack. I don't deserve the position of alpha.

I force myself to stay, even though I'd rather walk on, immersed in my thoughts about Sedona. "How's it going?" Yeah, it's lame, but I don't really know how else to shoot the shit with the guy.

He nods his head. "It's going. Almost finished with harvesting this year's crop. Then moving onto the cacao."

"Good." That's all I can think of to say, but I'm thankful when his name comes to me—Paco.

A woman comes out of the hut and shades her eyes as she looks in our direction. She walks up the hill and stands beside the old man. Must be his mate.

"Alpha," the old woman inclines her head. "Is it true?" She's wearing a dress that looks straight out of the 1950s. It probably is, actually. Some secondhand find shipped over as a donation from the United States. I look over at their hut, where a curl of smoke comes from the chimney. The hacienda has every luxury imaginable and these people don't even have electricity. I knew things were bad, but this makes me sick. What sort of alpha leaves his pack in poverty?

"Hush, Marisol," Paco admonishes.

"Is what true?" I brace myself for whatever is being said about me. That I'm mad or that I let my mate go.

"You hit Don Santiago?"

Oh that. Yeah. I shove my hands in my pockets. "It's true. The council and I are in disagreement about some actions they took." Right. I doubt I'm projecting the confidence I mean to, but it's the best I can muster when my mate is on a van driving miles away from me.

"Be careful, Don Carlos." Marisol's voice wavers, but I can't figure out why. Is it out of fear? Or ire? Is my pack ready to mutiny against me?

I growl. Not to scare her, but my pack needs to know I won't be cowed.

She takes a step back and her husband grasps her elbow to steady her.

"The council has overstepped." Ice infuses my tone. "They will not insult me or my mate without retribution."

Marisol and her mate both wear unreadable expressions. They probably think I'm the enemy, allowing them to live in poverty while I travel and attend the best universities. I don't blame them. That's exactly what I did. I don't deserve to be their leader.

No one speaks for a beat, so I nod curtly and walk on.

"May the fates accompany you." Paco's benediction makes me stop and look back. He and his wife lift their palms in a wave.

I return it.

I don't know how I'm going to do it, but things have to change around here. Clearing this cesspool feels urgent. I'm sure that reason has something to do with Sedona, but I don't even dare admit what my heart is pattering on about.

Fix it for her.

That's mad. Sedona's not going to come back here. Not in a million years. To entertain the fantasy is pure lunacy.

~.~

SEDONA

I LEAN my head against the airplane window and stare down at the fluffy clouds below us. Garrett, followed by most of our pack bum-rushed the airport last night in time for him to find Amber, his mate. In front of all of us, he declared his love and his intention to make up for his mistakes with her and she allowed herself to be reclaimed.

Now, they sit in the seats beside me, fingers intertwined, her blonde head on his shoulder. If it were up to me, I would've given them some privacy—have them sit next to a stranger so they can wrap into themselves, but Garrett insisted his pack member, Trey, book me a seat beside him. I guess so he can send me concerned glances every so often.

"Stop it," I snap when he does it again.

"Stop what?"

"Looking at me as if I'm broken."

Garrett grimaces. "I guess I just don't know what to do to help. Short of going back and tearing throats out."

"That's what you did to the guys in the warehouse? The ones who kidnapped me?" I both want and don't want to hear the answer to this.

Garrett scrubs a hand over his face. "Yeah. I lost my shit because Amber was there and my wolf needed to protect her. I killed everyone before we questioned them. Thank the fates it didn't keep us from finding you, or it would've been my fault completely."

"Carlos called them traffickers. Said he'd heard there were shifters selling shifters but hadn't believed it. What do you think they're selling them for? It can't all be sex traffic because they had a male shifter in a cage when I was in the warehouse."

"Yeah, they captured us when we first showed up and put us in cages, too." Garrett tugged on his ear like he was embarrassed. "Amber picked the locks to get us out. But I did wonder why they didn't just kill us."

"They were shifters themselves, right? Not humans who want to study our genes or something."

"Smelled like shifters to me, although I didn't see any of them shift. They had guns they probably thought would work to defend themselves. I killed them before they had a chance."

"What if they're shifters unable to shift? Carlos said his pack is full of them from too much in-breeding. I forget what he called them—defectives or something. That's why their council bought me—to rejuvenate the bloodline."

"Carlos. Is that his name? The guy you didn't want me to kill?"

Oh lordy. Just hearing his name brings on a rush of pain. I duck my head. "Yeah."

Garrett reaches out and touches my knee. "Did he hurt you, sis?"

The victim cloak falls on me like a smothering blanket. I struggle unsuccessfully to free myself of its confines and my eyes fill with tears. "No."

"But he marked you?" Garrett clears his throat, obviously uncomfortable talking about sex with me, his little sister. "Claimed you?"

"Yeah." My voice comes out as no more than a whisper.

"You can tell me, Sedona."

I try to swallow down the lump in my throat. "I was jogging on the beach when this guy approaches. Shifter. He says something to me in Spanish, which I can't understand,

and the next thing I know, there's a dart in the back of my neck and I'm on the sand looking up at four shifters. They put me in a cage and on a plane. I was in and out—I think they re-dosed me with the tranquilizer a few times. I woke up in the warehouse, and then they took me in a van to Carlos' pack where they sold me to two older men. They sedate me again to get me out of the cage and I wake up in a cell, chained to a bed. I have no idea how they got me to shift back to human form, but the last drug seemed different from the other tranquilizers."

Garrett is growling, eyes glowing silver and I shoot him a warning look. We're on a plane full of humans. I purposely left off the "naked" part because I knew he'd go berserk.

"Maybe we should talk about this later."

"No," Garrett snaps, pulling his alpha obey-me-or-else tone on me. "Tell me now."

"I will, if put your wolf away." I'll obey, but I won't be treated like a child. It's time for my father and brother to learn that.

Amber's fingers squeeze his and I'm soothed, knowing he's taken a mate who obviously cares and supports him.

Garrett cracks his neck, like he's about to go into a fight. "I'm in control."

I snort, but continue. "The door opens and Carlos enters. He acts shocked and walks over to free me and they lock him in."

Garrett's eyes narrow and I know what he's thinking. It totally could've been a setup.

"He shifts out of rage and tears around the room for a while, but they don't open the door. They keep us in there together over the full moon until we mated, then they hit us both with tranquilizers. I woke up locked in a bedroom upstairs. Carlos sent the boy to set me free when you guys showed up."

Garrett's face crinkles into a grimace but it seems he has no words.

Amber supplies them. "No closure. That must make it even harder."

I blink back tears, grateful she identified my malaise. I shouldn't need someone else to tell me why I'm so mixed up, but I do. "Yeah," I choke.

"You have to tell me something." Garrett's frowning. "Was it rape, Sedona?"

My face grows hot. I shouldn't have to talk about my most intimate moments with members of my family like this, but I get it. Garrett's going to go back and kill Carlos if I say *yes*. I'm glad I don't have to lie. "No."

His shoulders relax a bit. "So you believe he had nothing to do with it? He was a victim like you?"

"Don't call me victim."

Garrett studies me. "Sorry."

"Yes, I think so, to answer your question. But I'm not positive. If he were in on it, why would he let me go?"

"Because we were going to kill every last one of them and he knew they'd lose you anyway?"

My solar plexus tightens. "Right. That's a possibility."

Garrett turns to his mate. "Do you get anything on the guy?"

I don't understand what he's asking her at first, but Amber closes her eyes and I remember that he said she's a psychic. Daggers of anticipation stab me. Do I want to hear her answer? What if she tells me Carlos was a fraud? My stomach turns just thinking about it.

Amber shakes her head and I hold my breath. "I don't know."

Thank the fates.

She leans past Garrett to look at me. "I don't suppose you have anything of his that I could hold? We found that helped when I was trying to locate you."

"No, nothing." I left with nothing but the stupid night-dress thingy they put me in. Fortunately, Garrett brought my suitcase from San Carlos so I don't have to fly home in it.

Trey's head appears from the row in front of us. "What about the mark? His essence is embedded there."

Nice to know our conversation was completely un-private. I should have remembered my brother's pack members were right in front of us and could hear every word. Shifter hearing picks up far more than human ears can detect. *Oh well.* There's rarely any privacy in a pack, anyway.

I cover my healing wound and lean toward the window, away from Amber, even though she hasn't reached for me. I don't want to hear what her psychic abilities tell her.

"It's okay," she says softly. "I don't think you should trust my visions to make any decisions, anyway."

Garrett frowns. "Your visions are the reason we found Sedona. We trust them. You should, too." He reaches up to rub away the line between Amber's brows. The gesture is sweet and it makes me smile. I love seeing this side of him. I always knew my brother would make a great mate, but he'd never been interested in claiming a female until now. He could've had the pick of any litter—in any pack, but he only went through the motions when our father held inter-pack mating games up in Phoenix.

And no, they never let me participate, not that I had any interest, either.

Trey shrugs and turns back around. He's like a second brother to me—all of Garrett's pack members are. I'd trust them with my life, know they'd do anything for me, any time. But it's not because they care so much about me. it's because of whose sister I am. Up in Phoenix it's because of whose daughter I am. That's why hanging out with humans in college had been so refreshing for me.

Except when I think about my friends now, it's with total emptiness. I can't explain any of this to them. What would I say?

Pressure builds behind my eyes and nose as the confining net of victimhood descends again. Hot tears sting my eyes.

"Hey." Garrett grasps my nape but I shake him off. "What is it?"

"I don't want to go back to school," I choke. I only have one quarter left. It would be stupid not to finish, but the idea of returning to the silly farce I'd been living, pretending to fit in with humans, makes me physically ill.

I texted my human friends this morning to let them know that I'm okay, and that I had a harrowing experience with some Mexican drug lords, but that I need some time to recover. Away from Tucson. It's not true, but I don't want them showing up at my door with sympathy on their faces, making me out to be the victim.

"Okay. You don't have to."

Our parents might have something different to say about that decision, but Garrett holds my gaze, brows lifted with finality. I see a promise in his eyes. Somehow, he dealt with our dad up on the mountain. Made him listen and not fight. I don't know how he did that, because our dad's the world's biggest alpha-hole. But Garrett's bigger now. Younger. The days of my dad kicking his ass are over. Maybe the power has shifted. I was surprised he accepted Garrett's choice of mate without ripping into him.

"What *do* you want to do, sis?"

"Backpack across Europe," I blurt.

Garrett blinks at me. I bite my lips. What was I thinking? I can practically see him trying not to say "*no fucking way.*" I mean, he barely let me go to San Carlos for spring break and look how that turned out for me. The idea of them letting me tool around Europe on my own is laughable. And, yeah, even though I'm twenty-one years old, I'm still looking to my folks and Garrett to "let" me do things. Of course, they do support me—I live in one of the apartment buildings Garrett owns, and my parents pay all my other expenses.

Only you can live your life. You should be free to make your choices. The best advice I ever got, delivered to me in a dungeon by a man more imprisoned by tradition and pack history than I'll ever be.

Promise me.

Garrett arrives at his decision. "That's not going to happen."

Shocker. I turn my head to the window to end the conversation. I might not be locked in a cell anymore, but I'm still an overprotected pack princess. I'll never be free.

~.~

Council Elder

.   .   .

"How did the Americans find us?" I ask the four wrinkled faces of my fellow council members gathered in the meeting room. The trail should have been untraceable.

Don Jose snips the end of an eight hundred dollar Cohiba cigar and lights it. It's Cuban, from a limited edition box produced in 2007. I know, because I'm the one who bought it at auction last year for council meetings. Jose slides the box to the man at his left. "Through the traffickers. Or the Harvester."

Not the Harvester. Probably the traffickers.

"I'll go down to *el D.F.*"—what Mexicans call Mexico City—"to pay them a visit." I don't mention that I've already tried calling them in Mexico City. Relentlessly. The Americans stopped there first, I fear. So either someone sold us out, or they're all dead.

If it's the former, they'd all be dead by the time I finish with them. But I'll give them to Carlos, to appease his thirst for vengeance. Hell, I'll take him there myself and watch him do it. It will be good for my research to watch him in action. I haven't seen the alpha fight yet.

"What about the boy? He didn't fight to keep her." Don Mateo takes his turn with the cigar box, holding one up to his nose and inhaling deeply. "Do you think he's not truly bonded?"

It's indicative of how little power Carlos has here that we call him *the boy* rather than *the alpha*. But we need to be careful. He's angry with us now, which may cause unforeseen ripples. I would have preferred a much simpler plan with *in vitro* fertilization procedures.

"I think Carlos may be more valiant than selfish." I pace the room. "He may have wanted to spare our pack's blood."

"Or his own," Don Mauricio says drily.

"No. He's not a coward. The boy is intelligent." He is my

great-nephew after all. "His American business college taught him to strategize. He made the best decision he knew how to protect both the girl and the pack. Don't think he won't go after her when the dust settles."

"Do you know which servant set her free? Juanito?" Don Jose asks.

"Yes, but leave it. Carlos will protect him from punishment and we don't want to anger the alpha any more. If the only pack member in his corner is a nine-year-old boy and a crazy mother, we could do worse."

The men around the table chuckle with me.

"I'll take Carlos to the traffickers. Let him win this round. He's had his say and his way. He'll go after the female and bring her back, hopefully pregnant with his young."

"How can you be sure?"

I lift my shoulders. "He's an alpha male at the peak of virility. His wolf will demand he be near her."

"And if he chooses to stay away?" Don Mateo asks.

I smile. "All the better. We only need his young."

And I would love to keep his body for experimentation.

6

C *arlos*

I SIT in my mother's bedroom and watch her move around the breakfast food on the tray in front of her. Her eyes are glassy, face pale. It's been three interminable days since Sedona left. Three days, one hour and forty-three minutes, to be exact.

Maria Jose, Juanito's mother, pours me a fresh cup of coffee, milky and smooth. I love the coffee grown here on our mountain. I've been drinking it since I was a pup. It's mild enough I can drink it all day long.

"When is your father coming in?" my mother asks me.

My chest tightens, as it always does when she forgets he's dead.

"He's gone, Mamá. It's just me now."

I see a flicker of terror in her eyes before it fades and she bends her head to her buttered bread.

"I... found a female, Mamá." I surprise myself. I didn't expect to talk about Sedona, but she's occupying every part of my mind. My mother doesn't understand what I'm saying half the time, but she does now.

She lifts her head and stares at me.

"She's American. Her name is Sedona. Very beautiful." Beautiful doesn't do her justice. Exquisite. Mind-blowing. A perfect ten. She's magical.

My mother stands up as if Sedona is here and I jump to my feet and put a hand on her shoulder, gently pressing her back into her chair. "She's not here now, Mamá." I sit again and pick up my coffee cup, staring into it as I swirl the contents. "I don't know if she'll come back, actually." There. I admitted it. The dreadful truth I don't want to even look at. "She didn't want to be mated."

To my horror, tears spring into my mother's eyes and her lips begin to tremble. "I didn't want to, either," she says.

Oh fates. Why did I open this can of worms?

"I know, Mamá. That's why I would never ask her to stay if she doesn't want to be here."

Tears fall freely from my mother's chocolate brown eyes onto the breakfast tray. "Why can't I go home?" she wails.

"Mamá." I reach across the little table and cover her hand with mine. "Because we can take better care of you here. And I need you—your son," I say, in case she's forgotten who I am. "Carlos needs you."

She breaks into a sob. Fuck. I shove my chair back and walk around to put my arm across her shoulders. "Carlitos." She moans my name like a lament. "My only son."

My mother had five other pregnancies, but no others came to term. And I've been gone all these years., leaving her alone with a pack she never felt was hers. I'm a terrible son.

I look over at Maria Jose for help and she immediately comes forward. "It's all right Doña Carmelita. You're just sad because you haven't had your pills yet today." She picks up a little cup of prescription medications from the tray and shakes them so they rattle around. "Take these and you'll feel better."

My mother shoves them away, scattering the pills on the floor and Maria Jose drops to her knees to collect them. I help her.

"Does she usually take them willingly?"

Maria Jose shrugs. "Sometimes. I never know how she will be."

"What happens when she won't take them?"

"I hide them in her food if I can. If not, they have shots I can give her, but she hates that."

I drop the pills I collected back in the cup Maria Jose holds. "Thank you." I catch her eye and hold it. "You've taken care of her for all these years. I am grateful to you."

"Don Carlos..." Maria Jose glances toward the door, then back to me.

"Yes?"

"What if..." She draws in a breath. The fingers gripping the cup of pills turn white with tension. "What if these aren't what she needs?"

I stare at her, trying to understand what she's saying. "You think they're the wrong meds for her? They do more harm than good?"

She bobs her head. "Maybe there's a way... you could check?" She darts a glance at the door again.

"I'll ask Don Santiago," I say, moving toward the door. Don Santiago, my grandfather's brother, has a Ph.D. in biochemistry. He's not exactly a doctor, but he acts as the medical consultant to the pack.

"No!" Maria Jose grabs my arm, the whites of her eyes flash with panic. She immediately releases my arm, no doubt realizing how inappropriate it is for her to grab an alpha. Ducking her head, she tilts the cup of pills back and forth with a shaky hand. "Someone else," she whispers. "Not from the pack. Take her to the city. To America. Don't ask Don Santiago."

My skin prickles with what she's not saying. It's my turn to grip her. I grasp both her upper arms and squeeze until she looks up. "Why shouldn't I ask Don Santiago?" There's menace in my voice. I don't mean it toward her, but my aggression comes out at the suggestion that the wolf treating my mother might not be trustworthy.

Poor Maria Jose twists in my grasp. "Please, *señor*. It's nothing. Forget what I said. I beg you."

"No, Maria Jose. Tell me. You think I should ask someone besides Don Santiago. Why?"

Maria Jose blinks rapidly, still shifting against my grasp on her. I ease my clenched fingers, fearing I bruised her. "I am stupid," she mutters, but it sounds more to herself than to me. "I meant nothing by it. Do not consider the words of an idiot servant." She yanks again against my grasp and this time I let her go.

Ropes of unease twist in my stomach. There's something going on here I don't like. Not at all.

I watch, my mind whirling as Maria Jose coaxes my mother, docile now, into taking her pills. I consider my options. Wolves don't generally require a doctor's care, as we heal quickly and rarely suffer disease, but there may be some kind of shifter physician in the United States. I just don't know.

I kiss my mother on the head and leave for my room, which doubles as my office. In the days since Sedona left,

I've been making lists and rearranging the plans and ideas I had for the growth and modernization of Monte Lobo. Most of it requires money, which means I need to investigate the finances of the pack, figure out what we have available to spend. The trouble is, I've asked the council for the accounting five times and have yet to receive anything.

I also haven't decided what to do about the damn council. I need to strip them of some of their power, punish their actions against me. But before I do that, I need to truly understand all the dynamics afoot here. I don't have any support from the pack members, and why should I? I haven't been here to lead them. And without the pack, with the council calling me as crazy as my mother, I could easily wind up in that fucking cell again. Or dead. But that part doesn't worry me. It's thoughts of my mother's safety that has me cautious. The council can be vicious—I've seen it before.

I remember once, as a boy, smelling the blood from their meeting room as they called pack members in for untold crimes. There was secrecy and fear to the proceedings. Whispers and terror. My father had been away. When he came back, I remember him shouting at the council, arguing with them for hours, but nothing happened.

Had he been as ineffectual as I am against them? Why? How long has this form of pack rule been in place on Monte Lobo? Because it sure as hell isn't wolf nature. No other packs in the world are run this way, as far as I know.

But just because things have always been this way doesn't mean I can't change them. I just need to be smart. Have a plan.

I rub my face as I walk to my room. It's the master suite of the hacienda, the room that used to belong to my parents.

They gave it to me when I returned as an empty symbol of my alpha status.

I stand at the window and stare out. It's hard to get my brain to focus on anything besides Sedona. I still imagine I smell her on my fingers, taste her on my tongue. The image of her smile, her lovely long legs, that perfect body, plays in front of my eyes over and over again.

I hear her husky voice. Dream of claiming her over and over again, all night long. My days are an endless torture of Sedona memories.

And I can't stand that I haven't even spoken to her since she left. I don't even know her last name. Her phone number. Her address. But it's better this way. What would I say, after all? *I'm sorry my pack held you prisoner. I never want to do that to you, so have a nice life?*

I sigh and stab my fingers through my hair.

A knock sounds at my door. "Come in."

Don Santiago opens the door and saunters in.

I turn back to the window. "When will you produce the traffickers?"

"I can't get them by phone. It's possible the Americans already took care of them. I have the address of their warehouse if you want to check it out."

I'm both surprised and suspicious by this offer. Why wasn't it made initially?

"Where is it?"

"In *el D.F.*" Mexico City. That tracks with what Sedona told me.

"When will you look in on your female?"

I jerk around, surprised by the assumption in the question.

"If she's pregnant, you'll have to take responsibility for the child."

Pregnant. I'm sure the blood drains from my face. Why hadn't I considered the possibility? Sedona could be carrying my pup right now. She may need me. These past few days I thought I was doing her a favor by staying away, but what if I'm actually not owning up to my duty to her? If she's carrying my child, I owe her my support, my protection.

Sedona, pregnant. Oh fates. The thought makes me want to run and howl, whether from joy or desperation, I'm not sure. All the itchiness to be near Sedona comes screaming to the surface. I've been fighting it, but now, with this thought of my beautiful female alone, abandoned and pregnant, I can't stay still.

I fly into motion, packing a suitcase before I've even admitted to myself what I'm doing.

"I will take you into *el D.F.*, I have an errand there," Don Santiago says casually. "You can check out the warehouse before you go."

I've just been played and I don't give a shit. I can't think of anything except getting to Sedona. I need to find her, verify she's safe, and make her every promise she deserves. I will be there for her. I will provide. Protect.

Whether she wants it or not.

~.~

SEDONA

. . .

I PARK my Jeep outside Garrett's apartment building and get out. It's a Friday night, so Garrett should be working at his nightclub, but with a new mate, he might be home. I'm not here to see him, though. That's the point of coming on a Friday night. I want to talk to Amber, his mate. Because in addition to my mind twisting around and around what happened between Carlos and me, I have a new anxiety. A huge one. A looming question I would have to wait a week or two to get an answer on... unless I were psychic.

I enter the building and take the elevator up to the fourth floor. I know Amber's apartment is next door to Garrett's. I'm assuming they're staying there, since Garrett lives with Trey and Jared, and I doubt Amber wanted in on that frat party.

I scent Amber inside the door to the left of Garrett's and I knock. I hear her on the other side and I don't catch Garrett's fresh scent. "Amber? It's Sedona."

The door swings wide. "Sedona." Amber's blonde hair is pulled up into a French twist and she's still wearing her work clothes, looking sexy in a silk blouse and pencil skirt. Seeing her like this, it strikes me again how she's not the kind of female I would have thought Garrett would pick. She's sleek and refined where he's all rough edges and brute force, but her warmth is real as she invites me in.

"Garrett's not here, but he was going to try to come home early."

"That's okay. I came to see you, actually."

She doesn't seem surprised. I guess psychics know when you're coming.

"Do you want something to drink?" She walks over to the refrigerator in her bare feet and pulls it open. "I don't have much, but there's some ginger ale Garrett brought over. And beer." She looks quizzically over her shoulder.

"Ginger ale sounds great." I accept the frosty bottle and Amber grabs an opener out of a drawer. She pops hers first and passes it to me and I trade her for the one in my hand.

I look around her apartment. It's sparkly clean but not neat, if that makes sense. No dirt or dust, but there are papers scattered on the desk and a pair of high heels unceremoniously discarded by the front door.

"So, um... how are you feeling?" Amber asks.

Ugh. This is definitely not the conversation I want to have, even though I know she's genuinely asking and seems to care about my response. I draw a breath and launch into why I'm here. "I know I didn't want you to, um, use your abilities to tell me anything about Carlos, but..." I swallow. It's harder to say than I expect. "I just wondered if—I mean, I started worrying—" I walk around her living room, not able to face her directly.

"Yes." She whispers it, and it flips every hair on my arms.

But I don't even know if she's answering the right question. I whirl around and stare at her.

She flushes, uncertainty creeping over her expression, as if a direct mirror of my feelings.

"Yes, I'm pregnant?" I blurt.

She flushes deeper and nods. "That's what I saw."

I clutch a chair back to keep from falling over. The room spins around me and the floor possibly tilts as well. I don't know what I think or feel, but my gut believes she's right. My gut knew two days ago, I just didn't allow myself to listen.

Crap!

"Are you sure?"

The doorknob turns and I curse inwardly as Garrett's hulking form comes through, carrying a box of takeout food. "Sure about what?" His voice is sharp.

Of course he heard, he's a shifter.

"Did you tell him?" I ask weakly, still holding onto the chair to stay upright.

Amber's gaze darts from me to Garrett. "No."

Garrett stalks over, crushing the box of takeout in his hand. Someone who didn't know my brother is a giant teddy bear to the women he loves might be afraid. His pack members would straighten up to see the silver glint in his eyes. I'm not scared, though, and neither is Amber, although I sense her discomfort. She steps forward to salvage the box of food, shifting it swiftly to the counter before all the contents dump from the mangled cardboard.

"Tell me what?"

I force myself to breathe.

Amber doesn't answer, probably respecting my right to tell him or not.

My hand moves to protect my lower abdomen and Garrett's eyes widen.

"Oh fuck." He falls back and drops onto the couch. "I need to sit down."

"Me too," I manage.

Garrett scrubs his face. "Oh kiddo. I should've thought of this possibility. I was just so worried about getting you free and your mental state."

"I know," I croak. "Me too."

Garrett lifts his face from his hands and jumps to his feet, stalking over to me. He takes both my elbows. "I'll stand by you, whatever you decide to do."

I tug away from him, hating the close scrutiny. I appreciate what he's saying, but my mama wolf growls at the suggestion I do anything but keep my pup.

But will I be able to keep him or her?

I moisten my lips. "Wh-what do you think Carlos will do if he finds out?"

My brother's lips tighten and his chest expands and I know he'd do anything in his power to protect me or my pup from any threat. "If he even tries to take that pup from you—"

"You think he will?" I cut in.

Garrett's lips tug downward. "Every mated male wolf needs to protect his female. Multiply that need by one hundred for an alpha male. And an alpha male with a pregnant female?" Garrett shakes his head. "It would take an entire pack to keep him away."

I should have let Garrett hold onto me, because the floor tilts sideways again. My blood plummets to my feet. I can't put Garrett's or my father's packs at danger. But maybe Carlos won't find out. He hasn't come looking for me yet—hasn't made any attempt to contact me. Maybe I can keep the fact that I conceived a pup a secret from his pack.

"I'm moving you into this apartment building. It's where I wanted you from the start," Garrett declares.

I remember the argument. I'd begged him to let me stay in one of his buildings closer to campus—and further from his watchful eye. He'd relented, because even though he's an overprotective alpha, he's also a sweetheart.

"I—" I start to argue, then change my mind. Better not to tell him what I'm thinking. "Okay."

Garrett's shoulders sag. "I'll get the pack over first thing tomorrow. Don't worry—they'll do everything. You don't have to worry about a thing, okay, kiddo?"

I nod, but I'm already heading out the door. "Okay, thanks. Thank you, Amber." I turn the doorknob.

"Maybe you should stay in my place tonight," Garrett says.

I knew that was coming.

"No, I'll be fine. Tomorrow is soon enough. Good night." I leave before he can think about it any harder.

Carlos may come looking for me, and if he does, I need to be long gone from Tucson. In fact, I'm safer if no one knows where I am.

~.~

CARLOS

I LURK in the shadows of Sedona's apartment building like a thief.

I guess I am a thief waiting to steal—what? Sedona's heart? Her body? *Carajo*, I'd settle for a few minutes of her time.

She isn't home at the moment, though. Finding her took little effort. Rather than ask around in the shifter community, which would alert her brother's pack to my presence, I searched for the word *Sedona* and *University of Arizona art* until I found a mention of an art show she participated in and discovered her last name. From there, I researched until I found an address, which I prayed was still current. Judging by her scent lingering around an upstairs apartment, it is.

Now, just being close to where she lives, close to seeing her, my flesh pricks with anticipation. I can't get the image of her swollen, freshly kissed lips out of my head. Or the way her lashes fluttered just before she came. And oh, fates, her taste. I'm dying to get between those beautiful thighs again and lick her until she screams.

My Sedona.

A Jeep pulls up and I know before I even see the figure behind the wheel that it's her. She climbs out, looking every inch the goddess of youth and fertility. Her chestnut hair is pulled back in a thick ponytail that swings when she walks. She's wearing a pair of short shorts, her long legs tan and sleek. Oh hell, the curve of her ass almost shows in the back where they're cut off. A low growl rumbles in my throat thinking of all the males who have seen her dressed this way.

I don't think she heard me, but she tosses a glance over her shoulder and picks up her pace. I slink along the side of the building as she approaches the front door.

Fuck.

There's a key card to get in. It must only be locked at night, because I'd walked right in earlier. She slips through and shuts the door, peering out into the darkness like she knows I'm here.

Dammit. I freeze, ducking back into the shadows. When she disappears, I creep closer to check out the door situation.

I'm in luck. A couple comes out, arguing about something and I move swiftly forward, walking like I own the place, and catch the door. There's an elevator, but I take the stairs, calling on a little shifter power to mount them at full speed. I come out on the third floor at the same time the elevator opens. Sedona sees me and her eyes widen.

"Carlos."

I start forward, but her next words stop me in my tracks.

"Did the council send you?"

"What?" I swallow a growl. "No. Of course not." Even if

Santiago mentioned it, the idea was already in my head. "They're lucky to be alive, after the stunt they pulled. I came because I had to see you." I spread my hands. "It's just me, Sedona. I am alone."

I wish I could report to her that I avenged her kidnapping, but when I arrived at the warehouse, I found the place cordoned off with yellow police tape, and steeped in the scent of shifter blood. Santiago was probably right, her family's pack got there first.

Sedona nods slowly, but to my shock, she turns and bolts for her apartment like she thinks she can outrun me.

She should know better than to run from an alpha wolf. Stopping the impulse to chase is impossible for me. I'm on her before I can even send the impulse to my brain to hold back. I grab her at the door and band one arm around her waist, catch the wrist holding her key to the lock with the other.

Her scent doesn't help me get my wolf in check. It's like apples and sunshine, even better than I remembered. Intoxicating. I don't pick up the scent of pregnancy, but it would be too early. I bury my face in her shoulder, drag my lips up the column of her neck. My cock, already heavy from the mere sight of her, stiffens in my pants.

"Sedona, beautiful she-wolf, why are you afraid of me?"

She *is* afraid—trembling even—and that's the part that makes me a sick fuck for not letting go of her. But I can't make myself, because now that she's in my arms, I'm incapable of releasing her. Her back presses against my chest with each breath she takes, and I have the perfect view of her cleavage, rising and falling. I'm reassured by the fact that her nipples are hard, tenting her thin fitted t-shirt.

Her body remembers its master.

Drunk on the feel of her, I slide my palm inside her

shirt, up to one hand-sized breast, which I squeeze and knead, memorizing the weight, the size, the softness.

Her breath whooshes out on an exhale. "G-get off me." Her voice doesn't match the words and my wolf doesn't believe her.

"Do you think I would ever hurt you, beautiful?" I nip her earlobe.

The scent of her arousal reaches my nostrils and I breathe deep.

"N-no."

"Did you just want to make me chase you?" I bring the fingers of my other hand to cup her mons, pressing my middle finger into the seam of her shorts.

Her head falls back and she lets out a breathy moan that goes straight to my cock.

Even through the material of her shorts and panties, I note her growing dampness as I press my fingers against her heat. "I will always give chase, *ángel*." I scrape my teeth over her shoulder, over the place I marked her less than a week ago. "Because you belong to me."

She stiffens and I realize immediately my colossal mistake. "I do not belong to you." This time when she pulls away, I reluctantly release her. "Just because you marked me, doesn't mean you own me. *That's* why I ran."

She shoves her key into the lock, but her fingers tremble too much to get it in the first time, giving me a few precious seconds to try to regain footing.

"Sedona. I'm sorry." I slap my hand over the lock before she can try again. "That's not what I meant. My wolf is growling to reclaim you, that's all." I lean my other hand against the door, caging her between my arms, crowding her against the door with the heat of my torso. "I'm not so stupid or chauvinistic to think I have any rights to you. I came because I wanted to make sure you were all right. I couldn't stay away."

"Well, you're going to have to. I need space, Carlos." She turns, her soft curves brushing against my clothes, setting flames ablaze everywhere she touches. She puts a hand on my chest and tries to shove. She's an alpha she-wolf, so she's strong, but I still don't budge.

"Don't make me call my brother, Carlos. One word from me and he'll rip you apart."

I hate the direction this is going. I fucked everything up. Her brother might try, but I'm certain no wolf could keep me away from Sedona, if I'm under challenge. But I don't want to fight her family. "You could have sent him after me at Monte Lobo, but you didn't."

Her bravado cracks and pain flits over her face. "You let me go," she whispers.

I can't decide if she's thanking me or admonishing me. The idea that she wouldn't want to be released never occurred to me, and believing she might have been hurt by my actions makes me want to stab a knife through my chest. But she wouldn't have wanted to stay. That's impossible.

The agony of not knowing what she means makes me bold. Without touching her with my hands, I crush my mouth over hers, pushing until her head bumps the door. Once I have leverage, I lick into her lips, twisting mine and tilting my head for the best angle.

If she hadn't kissed me back, I would have retreated—no matter what my wolf wanted—but she melts into the kiss, her tongue meeting mine, lips moving against mine. Until she bites my lower lip, hard enough to draw blood.

I freeze as she holds it fast, tugging backward. When she releases it, there's a blaze of anger and defiance in her beautiful blue eyes. "Back off, Carlos."

I immediately retreat, hands in the air.

Fuck. *Stop thinking with your dick, asshole.*

"Sedona, please. No claims on you. I just want"—I rack my brain for right thing to say— "A date with you. Let me take you to dinner—to breakfast—anything. Meet me in a public place. I won't touch you, I just want a chance to be near you. To talk. Please?"

Sedona nods, but she's ducking her head back to the door, not meeting my eye. "Yeah, okay. Tomorrow night. Seven o'clock." She unlocks her door and steps into her apartment, clicking it shut without a backward glance.

My wolf fist pumps, but my brain knows better. She has no intention of meeting me tomorrow. She just said whatever it took to end the conversation.

I tunnel my fingers through my hair and stare at the tile floor of the hallway.

Carajo.

I won her body with the help of the full moon and a confined space. But how do I win her heart?

7

S *edona*

THREE A.M., my alarm goes off. I'm up, out of bed and dragging out my small purple rolly-suitcase. The same one I'd
taken to San Carlos just over a week ago. A lifetime ago.

If I were smart, I'd go to the bank and drain my accounts
to take cash, but there's no time. I found a flight to Paris at
quarter to seven, and I plan to be on it. I need to get out of
town, out of the country, *now*.

You should be free to make your choices, he told me. Yeah,
right. He may believe that in theory, but the minute Carlos
finds out I'm carrying his pup, I'll be lucky if he doesn't drag
me back to the dungeon cell himself. He won't be able to
help himself. Just like he couldn't keep from marking me.
Alpha wolves are dominant wolves. Possessive. Controlling.
Even domineering.

"He has no claim on me," I mutter, as I toss shirts and

changes of panties into my bag. A dress, a pair of boots. My lips tingle at the memory of his kiss, and I wipe the ghost of his touch away. "I was just a convenient piece of ass. I am not his mate." Ignoring my wolf's protest, I stuff another pair of jeans into the suitcase and zip it up. I have no clue what to pack for Europe, but I'm guessing they have places that sell clothes. If I need something, I can buy it. That's if my dad doesn't shut down my credit card to force me home.

Thank the fates I'd gone to the trouble of getting a passport to go to San Carlos.

My phone dings when the Uber arrives. I wave the driver off when he tries to help me throw my suitcase in the trunk and do it myself, then jump in the back of his car, twisting around to scan the area around us. No one is around, but the back of my neck prickles like I'm being watched.

I check in at the airport, buy a bottle of water and tell my racing heart to calm down. *There's no way he knows I'm here.* But telling myself that doesn't help. I can still feel him, as if he's just touched me and stepped away. I barely slept last night and when I did, my dreams were all of Carlos. My skin is itchy with the need to shift, as if I might be under attack at any moment.

But that's silly. Carlos wouldn't attack me. He said he just wanted to talk. Go on a date, like a normal couple.

What would it be like to date Carlos? The thought of sitting across from him at a candlelit table appeals more than I'd care to admit. If only we'd met under different circumstances. I indulge in a silly fantasy—Carlos is visiting the States, maybe setting up trade for his pack. We meet by chance—pass each other in a hallway, or he comes to my art show. No, he's ahead of me in line at Starbucks. He scents me, recognizes what I am and turns, his dark eyes glimmering with interest.

We flirt. He asks me to dinner. I'm charmed by him, attracted to his good looks, enthralled with his intelligence and accomplishments. He tells me about Monte Lobo.

Ugh. Or not. A happier topic, then. He tells me funny stories from his college days. Woos me into bed with him. My first time is jittery and exciting. He makes it ultra-romantic, pouring fresh wine into glasses. He's gentle and sensitive.

Hmm. Or not. Somehow this fantasy falls totally flat. I guess I prefer the wild roughness of the way he took me in Monte Lobo.

Did you just want to make me chase you?

A new fantasy floats into my mind. We're in the woods, but in human form. I'm running, he's giving chase. He tackles me to the ground, pins my wrists over my head as he shoves into me. I throw my head back, cry out at the mixture of pain and pleasure. He claims what he desires, so impassioned, he's unable to stop himself. I moan and writhe beneath him, resisting, but only because I love feeling his strength, having him hold me down and force me...

I squeeze my thighs to alleviate the pulse of heat starting there. Twitch them together when that doesn't work.

Damn.

I'll feel better once there's an ocean between us. I'll have some space and time to consider my options, decide how to proceed. Maybe when I get home, I'll allow Carlos to court me, as he suggested.

Except then what? Am I going to get serious with the male from a pack that *bought* me? That considers me a *prize* for their alpha? How would a relationship look? Would I move to Monte Lobo?

Never!

And I couldn't ask an alpha wolf to abandon his pack for me.

No, the best thing is to keep this pregnancy a secret and never have contact with Carlos again. Maybe when our pup reaches adulthood, I'll tell him or her the truth about how he or she was conceived.

But I have eighteen years to figure that part out.

For now, my decision is made. No more Carlos.

I may be marked, but it doesn't mean I can't find happiness with another wolf. One who will defend me and my pup against Carlos and his pack.

Why does that thought bring on a nasty wave of nausea?

Okay, maybe I won't find another wolf. I'll marry my art, find happiness that way.

Promise me.

I rub my chest as if I can will the ache away. It probably won't always hurt this bad. Will it?

~.~

Carlos

I buy a University of Arizona t-shirt and ball cap and after-shave at the airport sundry shop. I step into the men's room and slather the aftershave over my face, neck and hands to mask my scent. I change out of my button-down, wrinkled from the long night I spent dozing in my rental car outside Sedona's building. I purposely bought the red t-shirt in a size too large, so I won't call attention to my muscled shifter physique. Not that I think women will throw themselves at me, but I'd rather blend in as the average American today. Or average Mexican-American, of which there are plenty in Tucson. If I concentrate, I can even speak without any accent.

I rip the tag off the ball cap and pull it low over my eyes, then survey myself in the mirror. It will do. Now, I just need to remember to reapply the aftershave during the flight, and with any luck, Sedona won't scent me while I'm on the plane with her. All the way to Paris.

It was tricky to lurk behind her, close enough to over-hear her book her flight, but far enough away not to trigger her sensitive sense of smell, but I did it.

I adopt a casual walk as I head out of the bathroom and pass our gate, choosing instead to sit at the one across the way. The one that gives me an excellent view of my beautiful mate.

Her hair is loose this morning, spilling over her slender shoulders, framing her perky breasts. She's dressed in a pair of jeans that ought to be illegal on any female with an ass like hers and she's squeezing her thighs together like...

Fuck me! Is she pleasuring herself?

Sedona's cheeks flush and she continues to press her knees together, shifting her hips like she's turned on.

I almost fail to swallow the growl that rises in my throat as I cast my gaze around the seating area with a glare. Who has her turned on like that? I will fucking *kill* them.

But I don't see any male who would arouse her excitement.

It must be her own thoughts, then.

Could she be thinking of me?

That thought nearly brings me to my knees, the desire to

spread her creamy thighs and apply my tongue to the pink heart there so overwhelming it makes me dizzy.

Sedona. My beautiful she-wolf.

I shift to rearrange my straining cock in my jeans. I need her like I need air to breathe.

Thankfully, they call our flight, and Sedona gathers her things and stands. Another minute and I would've been on the floor between her knees.

Giving my presence away.

I pick up my bag and stand, entering the middle of the throng, blending in. We board the plane and somehow, I manage to pass Sedona without her noticing me. I take my seat across the aisle and back a few seats and pull my cap even lower over my face.

After the plane lifts into the air, Sedona pulls out a sketchbook and flips it open to a blank page. With quick movements of a black ink pen, she sketches something I can't see from where I sit.

I ache to know what she's drawing. I've never even seen my mate's art—that guts me. There's so much I don't know about her—what she likes, what she doesn't. Why she wants to go to Paris.

I don't even know what I'm doing. Somewhere, in the back of my mind, is the nagging thought that the council conveniently got rid of me before I made them pay for what they did to Sedona. Before I could interfere with the status quo that only benefits them. My pack needs me and I'm out of pocket again.

But my wolf compelled me to follow Sedona. Now I'm creeping around like a stalker, hiding in plain sight from my mate. What is my plan? To convince her to date me in Paris?

I actually scoff out loud.

If my presence in Tucson upset her enough to leave the

country, what makes me think she'll ever accept me after I've followed her halfway across the world? I came to find out if she's pregnant—to provide for her, and protect her.

But it's too soon to know if she's with pup, and she obviously isn't interested in my provisions or protection. Courting her isn't an option, either. She clearly doesn't want to see me. And I won't ever claim her against her will. So that leaves me where I am—lurking in shadows. Watching. Waiting to find out if she's pregnant. Ready to protect her if she needs me.

So what will I do if she is carrying my pup?

Consternation grinds in me.

My options totally suck.

Capture her. Or let her go.

Fuck.

8

G *arrett*

SEDONA DOESN'T ANSWER her phone or her door, despite the fact that her car is parked outside. A month ago, I would've shrugged such a thing off as another irresponsible college student move. But after what happened to her last week, my paranoia spikes sky high.

I pound on her door with my fist, cracking the solid wood. "Sedona!"

Trey and Jared shift behind me. The rest of my pack will be arriving in a few minutes to move Sedona's things to my building.

"You have a key, you know," Trey reminds me.

I curse and pull out my keyring, finding the master to the entire building and inserting it in the lock.

Inside, Sedona's apartment is a mess. Not a mess like it's been ransacked, just her usual chaotic disaster-area. She definitely hasn't put any effort into getting packed for the move, but I'd told her not to.

I look around the room, my skin prickling with unease.

"She left you a note, G." Jared hands me a piece of notebook paper with Sedona's hasty scrawl.

GARRETT,

I'm heading out of town for a while. Don't worry about me, I'm fine—just need some time alone to think and process.

I love you.

XXOO Sedona

I CRUMPLE the paper up in my hand and hurl it at the wall, unable to stop the roar of frustration that leaves my mouth.

Of course, my pack—minus my beta Tank, who is still tied up with the job I gave him of keeping a lid on Foxfire, Amber's best friend—chooses that moment to show up. They crowd into the room, their hulking bodies filling the small space until it feels like my nightclub on a Saturday night. I bark orders to get things packed up and loaded onto the truck and step outside to try calling my little sister once more.

It goes straight to voicemail. Just like last weekend. But she left a note this time. And she's probably not answering because she doesn't want me to stop her.

I pull out my phone, forcing myself to take a deep breath first to keep from crushing it in my palm. I send a text to Sedona, *Please call or text me to let me know you arrived safely.*

There. Not too intrusive, but clear and firm. The real problem will be keeping my dad from going ballistic. Like when she disappeared, I'm in the position of deciding how much information to feed him and when. And of holding him back from interfering, when my own instincts scream to go barreling after her and make sure she's safe.

But maybe there is a way to make sure. I pick up the crumpled note and shove it in my jeans pocket. "I'll meet you guys at her new place," I tell Jared and head outside for my motorcycle.

Amber hates being put on the spot as a psychic, but the more she practices using her gifts, the more she'll come to accept this magical side of her. And who better to push her than her new mate?

I speed back to my apartment building and find Amber still asleep in bed. Which is where she should be, considering it's a Saturday and I kept her up most of the night, screaming her releases until she went hoarse.

She rolls over, smiling and humming softly when I come into the room. Her naked body is twisted up in a lavender sheet and I can't resist the urge to yank it off and simply stare at what now belongs to me.

Amber leans up on her elbows, studying me. Not in the suddenly sex-addled way I'm staring at her, but with concern. As if she can read the emotion I brought in with me.

"What is it?"

I crawl over her and run my tongue over her still-healing wound from where I marked her. Unlike Sedona, whose bite mark closed immediately, Amber is human so her flesh doesn't regenerate as quickly as ours. My saliva helps speed the process, though.

She tilts her head to the side and makes that adorable humming noise again, but she keeps at me. "What happened?"

"Sedona's gone. She left a note that she's leaving town.

I'm guessing she's acting on her desire to see Europe." I pull the crumpled note out of my pocket and hand it to her. Not for her to read the words, but to sense the energy. We found this method worked in San Carlos with Sedona's clothing.

Amber takes it, but holds my gaze. "Maybe she needs some time to regroup. A change of scenery."

"I know. But I hate the thought of her all alone—unprotected. They might go after her—" I shut up when I see Amber's gaze lose focus.

She stares through me for a moment, then murmurs, "She's not unprotected."

I stiffen. "Who?" But I already know who and it makes me want to kill the motherfucker.

"Carlos is following—not to hurt her," Amber adds quickly, her focus returning to my face. "He needs to protect her, but I don't think he wants to compel her."

My most protective urges relax but I grumble as I settle beside my incredible mate. "I still don't like it."

Amber blinks several times before she speaks in a faraway voice, "The pregnancy ensures her safety... but not his."

~.~

Sedona

MY PHONE BUZZES with an incoming text. I set my sketchpad and pencil down on the bench I'm sitting on and fish the phone out of my purse. It's from Garrett. By some miracle, he hasn't sent some alpha bullshit message demanding I come home or hole up in my hotel room until he gets here. Instead, this text is a list of resources—the pack leaders in each country of Europe and where to find them or how to contact them. It's sweet, but totally unnecessary. I don't need help. Unless it's in the form of a date with a vampire to get my memory of Carlos scrubbed.

But then I guess I'd be pretty confused about how I got pregnant. Le sigh.

I haven't heard from my parents yet, which means Garrett must not have told them. My mom had planned on coming down to be with me in Tucson the minute I got home, but I talked her out of it, which I know hurt her feelings. I just don't want to be babied by my parents right now.

I rub a line on my sketch of the ancient statue *Winged Victory of Samothrace*. I added Nike's head and arms back in but created the drawing in simplicity—a children's book version of the Greek goddess. I have to say, her wings are exquisite.

Part of me feels like coming to the Louvre to sketch the art is too cliché—the art student studying the masters. But I actually forgot about Mexico and the pregnancy for a moment here, which is a gift.

A girl—maybe nine or ten—stops and looks over my shoulder. "Wow, mom—look, a real live artist is here!" She's American. Very cute.

"Shh, don't bother her, honey." Her mother has that indulgent tone that says she knows her daughter is no bother, but feels obligated to say something, anyway.

Humans have been looking over my shoulder all morning, murmuring their comments in various languages, but this one is the cutest. I tear the drawing out and hand it to her with a smile.

"Is this... *free*?" Judging by her look of incredulity, she thinks I'm on par with Michelangelo.

This is why I want to illustrate children's books. Or make greeting cards. Some artists would call commercial art a sell-out but for me it's not about making money. It's just the kind of art I like to make. The audience I prefer to reach.

"Yep. And it's just for you. What's your name?" I pull the drawing back and lift my pencil.

"Angelina."

I write *To Angelina, from Sedona, The Louvre* and the date.

She beams at me as she takes it. "Thank you very much." Her mom cradles her shoulder as they walk away. Angelina turns back. "Your English is really good."

I laugh and her mom looks embarrassed. "She's American, honey."

Out of nowhere, Carlos' scent fills my nostrils. It's happened at least a half dozen times a day since I left. I think it's because his essence is embedded in me now.

It could drive a she-wolf crazy.

Because I seriously don't know how I'm supposed to get over him when his scent assaults me at every turn. Even a continent away. Not that I ever forget, except that rare moment drawing. Everything reminds me of him. I remember the growl of his voice speaking low in my ear, of his large hands coasting over my skin. The way his eyes glowed amber when his wolf came to the surface.

And I wonder a million things about him. What it would be like to run with him in wolf form, what he would think of Paris, of my family, of my art. Will I be able to keep the news of this pregnancy from him and his pack?

I pick up my pencil and start to sketch again, only this time it's not Nike, it's a black wolf. He's snarling, teeth bared, fur standing up in a ridge down his back. When I finish, I smudge the fur around his ears and hold it at arms' length for perspective.

Goosebumps prick my skin. It's Carlos, but I don't know why I drew him this way. Do I think he's protecting me?

Or coming after me?

~.~

Carlos

I watch Sedona head into her hotel room and sag against a wall in defeat. Is it possible to go moon mad when you've already taken a mate?

Because I seriously can't stand being near Sedona but not with her. I'm feverish with the need to touch her, to get closer to her. I want to be the recipient of the smiles she reserves only for children. *Thank fuck* she doesn't smile at other males or they'd be dead before they hit the floor.

I know I'm not thinking straight. I'm drunk on need. I've forgotten what I'm doing here.

Or rather I've changed my mind a hundred times. Right now, my mind is set on winning Sedona back—not that I ever had her. But she'd been warming up to me back in that cell. If I could just get some extended time with her alone again, I know I can seduce my mate. The physical attraction is strong. We'll start with sex and build from there. I'll learn everything else about her and show her I can be the mate she deserves.

So. How to get her alone?

It's wrong. So wrong. But I'm an asshole enough to think I can pull it off. I head out of the hotel and find a sex shop. The kind that sells handcuffs. Bondage tape. Ball gags.

This could backfire horribly. Or it might be just the thing we need...

9

S *edona*

I STEP IN YET another puddle and rain water soaks my shoes and socks. It's rained all day and I'm not as excited as I expected to be walking along Montemartre tracing the steps of Picasso, Renoir, and Degas.

I don't even know how much of Paris I took in as I wandered the streets today. My chest aches like someone punched me. A few Frenchmen give me odd looks, and I realize my wolf is whining. The only time she's happy is when I think of Carlos—or fall asleep and dream of him.

This is Stockholm Syndrome. Right?

I stop at a sidewalk cafe to get some dinner and sink into a seat protected by a wide blue awning. Water pours from the edges, splashing my legs and gathering in little pools beside my table.

When rain comes in Tucson, we celebrate because the

desert is always thirsty, but today it just depresses me. I stare unseeingly at the menu. It hardly matters—I don't speak French and no one seems to speak English—or if they do, they don't bother to help me—so I've ordered *frites* and *chocolat chaud* or *cafe au lait* everywhere I've eaten. I'm going to get sick of French fries and hot chocolate soon.

Carlos' scent swirls around me again and sadness stirs behind my eyes. Part of me wonders what our date would've been like, if I'd stayed in Tucson and let him take me to dinner. He would have held the doors and paid, like a perfect gentleman. That much I know. But would we have found laughter together? Would we joke? Tease? Would the same sparks be there between us that we felt during the full moon?

Hah. How can I even doubt that? He couldn't keep his hands off me in Tucson, and he was trying to make amends.

I stare at the cafe across the street, not really seeing anything or anyone. Not until my eyes meet the gaze of a man who has the look of a spy stealing glances.

A jolt of electricity flashes through me.

Carlos.

The man looks away, playing it cool.

Wait, is it him? I can't tell now, because he's turned his face away. But it has to be. The man has the same broad shoulders, same dark hair and bronze skin.

Fuck. Me.

What in the hell is he doing here? Has he been following me this entire trip?

I resist the urge to stomp across the street and sock him in the face. No, he doesn't know he's been made yet, which gives me the upper hand. If he wants to follow, I'll make it exciting for him.

I finish my meal and pay the bill, then play entitled

oblivious American and walk right through the kitchen and out the back door, slipping into the alleyway behind the cafe.

Catch me if you can, I murmur through clenched teeth.

I have no doubt he'll find me soon, and I'm not feeling kindly toward him at the moment. But how to punish him for this incredible infringement on my privacy, my space?

Garrett's text yesterday said his contact in Paris could be found at a paranormal bar called The Dungeon. I don't care about meeting up with the contact, but a paranormal bar would be just the kind of place to get under Carlos' skin.

Normally, it wouldn't be a location I'd frequent alone. I've been warned my whole life about staying away from places like that. As a shifter, I'm fairly safe in a normal bar— no human man could mess with me unless he drugged me first. But a paranormal bar is full of trouble, and dangerous for a single female. Or maybe that's just the bullshit lie I've been fed all my life.

Either way, I have a feeling Carlos will lose his everloving shit at seeing me there, and that serves him right for stalking me like a creep-o.

I look up the location on my phone and, as luck would have it, find it's just six blocks from the boutique hotel where I'm staying. I grab a cab to go back to the hotel, certain Carlos will show up there when he realizes he's lost my trail.

Feeling almost cheerful for the first time since I arrived in Paris, I shower and put on the dress I packed. A red dress. With a short flippy skirt. I blow dry my hair and apply some mascara and lip gloss. It must be the pregnancy, because despite my low mood over the last week, I look radiant.

Carlos, eat your heart out.

I don a pair of black knee-high boots and march out of

the building with a flick of my umbrella and a toss of my hair. Now that I'm watching for it, I notice when the door opens behind me, sense the black wolf's presence behind me.

Did you just want to make me chase you?

Yeah, I guess I do. Because my wolf loves this game. I have a bounce in my step as I walk down the narrow, cobblestone streets in search of The Dungeon. I walk past it a few times before I locate an unmarked door at the bottom of a short set of steps. Well, of course the Dungeon is located below ground level. Guess that should've been obvious.

I stretch out a hand to the door knob, listening first to make sure I'm not trying to walk into someone's home or something. No, I hear music. I push the door open.

It's like the cliché in every movie, when the needle scratches off and the place goes quiet, everyone turns to look at me.

One of these things is not like the other. At least I hope not. Because the crowd inside is seedy. With a capital S. And I stand out like a bright, juicy grape in a pile of raisins.

Scents assault my nose—shifters of all kinds are here, along with vampires and whatever else is freaky in Paris. They look like they live in this bar, faces flushed red and pickled with alcohol use.

I'm one of three females in the place, and the other two are old shifters of some kind and not attractive. I pick my way toward the bar. Dirt coats the floors, the tables haven't been scrubbed down to the wood in ages, if ever.

Behind the bar, a short, disheveled man dries a glass with a dirty rag, openly staring at me like everyone else.

I swallow and swagger to the bar, nudging my way between two leering males who don't have the decency to move their limbs and feet out of the way for me. "I'll take a ginger ale," I say.

The bartender doesn't move, just keeps polishing the glass like I didn't say anything.

Maybe he doesn't speak English. I sigh and try again. *"Café au lait?"*

This time the bartender's lip curls and he shakes his head.

Well, peachy.

Even if I hadn't sensed Carlos come in, I wouldn't let this asshole's lack of hospitality chase me away. I plunk both elbows on the bar, like I'm going to stay awhile. "Well, what do you have?"

He pours a clear liquid from an unmarked bottle into a small glass and pushes it over to me.

It smells like rubbing alcohol. For all I know, it's a home brew. Maybe laced with the date rape drug for good measure. Probably what they reserve for every stupid female who finds her way in here.

I don't touch it.

A shifter with broad shoulders and a tight black t-shirt comes over and leans his elbow down next to mine, a broad smile on his face. I don't recognize his scent until I see the dragon tail tattoo curling around the side of his neck.

No. Way. I've never met one before.

Before Carlos I might have been impressed. The guy is big, good-looking and oozes male dominance. But all I can think is how much better-defined Carlos' muscles are, how much kinder his dark-lashed brown eyes appear.

And suddenly, I'm not so sure about my plan to strut in here and get under Carlos' skin. I don't *actually* want to make him jealous—not in the real sense of the word, and this guy might do that.

I try to take a step back, but I'm pinned by another guy to my left. Also dragon. They're hunting together.

The dragon murmurs something in French and I shake my head, twisting and looking around the bar with a forced nonchalance. Where did Carlos go?

The dragon frowns and picks up my drink, lifting it to my lips.

I turn my face away and some of it spills down the front of me, cold droplets trickling between my breasts. The dragon's eyes light on the droplets and he leans forward like he's going to lick them off. I shove at his head, trying to get his tongue away from my skin. His friend grabs me from the back, chuckling as he pins my arms behind me. I scream.

I see a flash of skin and hear the crack of bone on bone. The dragon shifter roars and leaps to his feet, rubbing his jaw, as two hundred pounds of angry wolf wedges in front of me.

Carlos.

I've bitten off way more than I can chew. I never meant for him to have to defend me or fight for me. I only wanted to rile him up a little. To reveal himself.

Now we're both in serious danger. In human form, Carlos might be an even match for this guy, maybe even for the guy and his friend. But if they shift, a wolf is no match for a dragon. Hell, the dragon could burn this place down with one roar.

The dragon behind me chuckles, but he's released my arms. "The she-wolf has a mate," he observes in English.

I grab Carlos' arm and tug him toward the door. "Carlos, it's all right. Come on, let's go."

Carlos won't stop growling, nor does he take his eyes off his foe.

I pull with all my might. "Carlos, let's go."

The dragons haven't moved to escalate the fight, but I have no doubt they will if Carlos keeps it up.

I change my tactic, and push in front of Carlos, as if I'm going to defend him. He immediately picks me up by the waist and tries to set me aside, but I don't go. I repeat the action of pushing my way between them. It seems to do the trick, because his brow furrows. I'm banking on the instinct to get me out of danger being greater than his need to prove himself in front of me.

Carlos picks me up again and carries me toward the door, only stopping to readjust and throw me over his shoulder when we're clear of the dragons.

Miraculously, no one follows, no one challenges him.

He doesn't say a word to me or anyone else as he shoves out the door and climbs the steps. The rain has stopped and mist curls around the buildings and lamplights. Carlos' breath puffs in and out at an angry cadence as his shoes hit the cobblestones.

A shiver of excitement goes through me.

I like him mad.

Of course that makes no sense. I don't even know how to analyze it, other than recognizing his take-charge display of male dominance curls my toes. Maybe I do feel a teeny bit guilty, too, for nearly getting him killed in there.

He marches all the way back to my hotel, not setting me down until the elevator doors close behind us. Then he drops me to my feet, spins me to face a wall, and flattens both my hands against it with one of his pressed over the top of them. His other hand crashes down several times on my ass.

Ouch.

And... *yum.*

My panties dampen, heart taps rapidly against the front of my rib cage.

Carlos, you devil.

"Never, never go into a paranormal bar alone," he clips, his accent thicker than usual.

The elevator stops on my floor. He pulls my hands from the elevator wall, whipping me around, making the skirt of my dress swing and flare. "Come."

He marches straight to my door, taking my purse from my shoulder and retrieving the key.

I ought to be enraged by the proprietary actions, but I'm not. I'm still finding his anger enticing.

I know, it's weird.

The moment the door swings open, Carlos points to the opposite wall. "Hands on the wall, like before."

I try to muster some fire, cocking a hip. "What right do you have—"

Carlos is upon me in seconds, shoving me back against the closed door, mouth pressing over mine in a searing kiss. His large hands roam over my body, find the zipper on the back of my dress and yank it down. The dress falls to my feet and I stand in my black lace bra and panties and black leather boots. Stunned.

"Panties off. Keep the bra and boots," he orders.

My tummy flutters with excitement. I'm not the least bit scared of this male—maybe that's crazy. But we've been through worse and he managed to be a gentleman. He may be angry now, but there's no sign of his wolf in his eyes, only dark promise.

Delicious dark promise.

Still, I don't move to obey him. Maybe I just want to see what he'll do. How far will he take this authoritative stance?

I'm right. He doesn't grow angry, instead his eyelids

droop and he adjusts his cock in his pants. "*Muñeca*, get into position like I told you."

My nipples harden. I'm sure he smells my arousal because heat blooms between my thighs. I'm too excited to refuse him, so I strut across the room in my bra and boots and panties and put my palms against the wall, ass out.

"Good girl." His purr hypnotizes. He walks up behind me and hooks his thumbs in the elastic of my panties. I expect him to tug them off, but he lowers them to just below my buttocks. "You don't want to take them off?" His lips are close to my ear. "Now you have to keep them up. Spread your legs, *ángel*. If the panties drop, I start the spanking over."

My pussy clenches at the word *spanking,* which somehow thrills me the most out of all the sexy things we've already done, mango fucking included. I widen my stance to stretch the panties between my thighs. It's half-humiliating, half-erotic. I love it.

But then Carlos' hand claps down on my ass, harder than I dreamed possible, and the fun is totally over.

I yelp and jump away from the wall. "Ouch! That *hurt.*" Shifters may heal fast, but it doesn't mean we don't experience just as much pain as your average human.

Carlos grabs my ass, fingers gripping the cheek he just marked with his palm. He brings his body right up against mine, snaking an arm around my waist to hold me tight. His thick cock presses against my belly, hard and insistent. "I know, *ángel*. I meant it to hurt." He eases his grip on my ass and rubs away the sting. "You must get back into position."

I don't know how he manages to make his bossy words sound so sexy. Is it the rough timbre of his voice? Or the way he holds his lips so close to my ear?

Still, I'm not falling for it. Not now that I know how hard he spanks. "No."

He nips my ear, then traces the shell with the tip of his tongue. "*Sí, mi amor.* I need to show you I care enough to do this. I won't let you put yourself in danger."

My heart beats double-time. I feel he's telling me something important but it's all mixed up in sex and pain so I can't quite untangle it.

"Now go back to the wall and put your hands on it. Tip that perfect ass back for me so I can paint it red. And next time you think of risking your safety, you'll remember how much I cherish you." He's massaging my ass with both hands now and I can't stop grinding my pussy down on his hard thigh pressing between my legs.

"Th-that doesn't make sense." I sound completely breathless.

"Doesn't it?" There's a smile in his voice. "We'll see if it makes sense when I'm done." He grips my arm and propels me toward the wall.

I'm too curious now not to obey. I put my palms on the wall and tip my pelvis back. The panties fell to the floor when I jumped back the last time, so my ass is bare, legs quivering as I wait.

~.~

GLORY TO THE FATES, Sedona is right here, offering herself up like the most delectable morsel in paradise.

She's beyond beautiful with my handprint painting her creamy skin, her thick chestnut hair falling in waves down her back. I take a mental snapshot, wanting to remember this image forever. The boots, the muscular thighs, her exquisite bare ass. I add it to the ones that haunt me from our shared cell in Monte Lobo.

I would've torn those dragons apart, limb from limb, if they'd challenged me for Sedona. I'm sure that's why they didn't. They would have caught my scent embedded in her skin and deciphered that she is mine. No smart shifter gets between a male and his marked mate, no matter what the species.

And all that aggression seeks redirection now. If Sedona showed fear or anger, I'd back down. But I can smell her interest. Her nipples are taut, her breaths make those perky tits rise and fall rapidly. And her eyes are glassy, like I've already fucked her.

She needs this. We both do. It will release my aggression, show her how worried I was.

I draw my hand back and bring it down with a resounding slap. She jerks, but incredibly, stays put this time. I spank her again, striking the other side, then pepper her perfect round globes with a volley of slaps that leave her breathless, panting.

Her ass looks so pretty with the blush of my handprints coloring the lower half. Just enough to warm it. As a shifter, the pain will only be momentary, fading completely within minutes.

I squeeze a handful of her ass in one hand and wrap a fist in her hair, tugging her head back. "What were you thinking?" I growl and land another hard slap to her backside.

She jerks, but my grip in her hair keeps her from moving. "I-I knew you'd follow," she confesses.

I go still. She'd known I was there. Of course she had. I'd

been so caught up in the moment, I didn't note her lack of surprise when I shoved in to rescue her at the bar.

"I just wanted to draw you out."

What does that mean? She wants me here?

I ease my grip on her hair and move into her line of sight, leaning my head against the wall. I need to see her face, try to understand. "You knew I was here? For how long?"

She nibbles her lower lip. "I saw you at dinner."

I can't help but smile. Clever little she-wolf. That's why she disappeared from the restaurant. I'd been frantic trying to figure out where she went after she paid her bill. With the rain, I couldn't catch her scent when I moved in to scout the building, but then I'd looked up and seen her climbing in a taxi.

I stroke my knuckles over her luminous skin, tracing the line of her cheekbone. "Were you angry with me, beautiful? I was just trying to give you space, but I needed to look after your safety, too."

She moistens her lips with her tongue, which sends my cock surging against my zipper. "I was angry, yes. A little."

Her eyes are dilated. I'd be a fool if I chose this moment for a heart to heart. My female is ripe for the plucking right now. Maybe my trip to the sex shop wasn't such a bad idea.

I pinch her chin between my thumb and forefinger and lift it. "So you punished me by putting yourself in danger?" I arch a stern brow.

Her lids droop like she loves being scolded by me. "I didn't mean to put us in real danger. I just meant to tease you. Make you jealous of the attention I might get in there."

My wolf growls at the suggestion of males giving her attention, but I don't want to miss what she's telling me. My mate was *teasing* me. That *can't* be a bad thing. It means she wants something from me—but what? Attention? A declaration of intent? The upper hand? Whatever it is, I'm taking it as a win, just as I'm taking this moment. I have my glorious mate nearly naked and trembling for me, legs spread, ass red, lips swollen from our kiss earlier.

"That was naughty, Sedona," I chide, stroking her hair back from her face. I lower my voice. "I'm going to have to punish you again."

I see the flare of excitement in her at the same time she turns and lunges away.

I catch her by the waist and haul her into the air, tossing her on the bed.

She shrieks, laughing as she rolls for the edge. I dive on top of her, tackle and pin her down.

"*Tsk tsk, ángel.* That earned you even more punishment." I can't stop the grin from stretching across my face. My wolf loves the chase as much as she loves to run. I hold her wrists down beside her head and take a moment to drink her in. So lovely. Her thick, glossy hair cascades in waves around her head, her cheeks carry a pretty flush of color.

I bend my head to her breasts and bite each nipple through the black lace of her bra, then fasten my teeth around the center of it and tug.

"Wait, wait, wait." Sedona struggles against my grip on her wrists. "I'll take it off, Carlos. Don't rip it. I love this bra."

"I do, too." I waggle my eyebrows and release her wrists, help her peel the straps down her arms and unhook the fastener in the back. I use the bra to wrap her wrists together, then I fasten them to the iron bedpost at the head of the bed. "Do not move, Sedona," I warn. "Or you'll rip your favorite bra. I will be back in two minutes."

"Wait!" She twists around, her eyes flying wide.

She doesn't like being left in such a vulnerable position.

Oh fates, I hope this isn't bringing back a bad memory. I'd only hoped to make good ones. I climb back over her and kiss the sensitive skin on the insides of her arms. "You know you can get out of this with little effort, right, *ángel*? I promise I'll be right back. Three minutes—tops. I just need to get something from my room. Okay, beautiful?"

She nods, visibly relaxing.

I unzip her knee-high boots and slide them off her feet, along with the thin nylon socks she wore underneath to make her more comfortable. To re-set the mood, I make my face stern. "You use this time to think about what your punishment should be, little white wolf. And we'll see if our ideas mesh when I return."

When she rolls her hips, I'm reassured she's not afraid or traumatized. My she-wolf likes what I plan for her. I take Sedona's key and slip out of the room to jog two floors down to mine, where I retrieve the bag of toys.

My eyes lock on Sedona the moment I walk in and I'm unable to look away. Everything about her is mesmerizing—the smooth cream of her skin, the peaks of her breasts. The flat, fluttering belly, her smoothly waxed mons. She watches me, twitching her thighs together like she needs relief. I definitely plan to give it to her. After a fair bit of torture.

"Oh, *ángel*." I quickly unbutton my shirt as I stalk to the bed. "I can't believe I left these perfect nipples unsucked." I shuck the shirt and climb over her, delighting in the shiver that runs through her body the moment my legs straddle her thighs. I flick one nipple with my tongue, once, twice, coaxing it into its stiffest peak. Then I latch my lips over it and suck, hard.

She moans and arches, throwing her head back, chin toward the ceiling.

"Lovely, lovely girl."

"Carlos." I love hearing her say my name so breathlessly.

"That's right, *ángel,* Carlos brings you pleasure. Only Carlos."

She wriggles, pants, whimpers. "No."

"No?" I stop torturing her worship-worthy nipple and lift my head.

She shakes her head then changes it to a nod. "Yes. Wait—"

I don't move. I know she's confused—hell, I'm confused, too. But I definitely don't want to move in for the kill if she's going to hate me afterward.

"Carlos—what are you doing?"

I crawl backward over her luscious body to settle between her legs. Sliding my hands under her buttocks, I lift her core to meet my mouth and take a long lick. "Punishing you."

Her entire body jerks and the cry that comes from her lips has me groaning with desire. My cock aches to be inside my beautiful mate.

"You deserve this punishment, don't you, beautiful? For being a terrible cock tease?" I flick the tip of my tongue over her clit.

She makes a sound resembling *ooh-ooh* as she thrusts her pelvis toward my mouth.

"That's it, doll." I suction my lips over her little swollen bud and take a draw.

She squeals, thrashing her legs around my ears.

"I have big plans for you, little she-wolf. And they all involve you naked and at my mercy."

Her pussy gushes moisture and it's all I can do to keep from yanking my dick out and sinking into her tight channel.

But I want to take my time with her tonight. My plan had

been to re-forge intimacy and that means drawing this out. Even if it takes all night.

~.~

SEDONA

SOMEWHERE IN MY brain lies the urge to protest this unexpected turn of events. I'd planned to punish Carlos with my red dress and appearance in a bar, now he's wrested all control from me.

But I'm not feeling weak. On the contrary, being the object of Carlos' singular focus, seeing the dark need and lust swirling in his gaze sends power coursing through me even though I'm the one tied up.

He takes another pull off my clit, then rolls me onto my stomach, taking care to adjust the bra binding my wrists to keep my arms comfortable.

My mind may have a few reservations, but my body's clearly on board with whatever Carlos is planning, because I lift my ass, giving him a better view of my most intimate parts.

"Mmm." Carlos grabs a proprietary handful of one cheek, squeezing roughly. "You keep that ass rolled back for me, *ángel,* show me you can take your punishment like a good girl."

My insides turn liquid, heat building in my core. I love Carlos' dirty talk—this game he's playing with me. I expect him to crawl up and enter me from behind—I crave that, actually, but I hear him rummage in the bag he brought and the flick of something plastic, like the flip of a lid.

When he pries my butt cheeks apart, I freak. Tugging on my bound wrists for leverage, I pull my knees up under me, and crawl away.

Carlos grabs my calf and pulls me back flat on my tummy. "Ah ah, *mi amor*. That's not taking it like a good girl." He tries again to prise open my cheeks, but I list to the side, rolling to press my ass to the bedspread.

Amusement lights Carlos' handsome face. He's on his knees beside me, holding a tube of lubricant in his hand, but he drops the lube and grasps both my ankles. Connecting them in one large hand, he holds them high and delivers several sharp slaps to my ass.

I shriek in surprise at the spanks and the shockingly vulnerable position, my ass in the air, lady parts exposed. Carlos tilts my legs toward my head and dribbles some lube into my ass crack.

"Carlos." I'm whimpering now. Anal sex is totally not something I'm prepared to give him, no matter how hot and bothered he has me.

He leans over and kisses my smarting cheeks. "Shh, beautiful wolf. You have nothing to fear from me."

The flutters in my belly say different, but as I analyze the statement, I know he's right. I trust this male not to harm me. Even so, I shake my head.

Carlos picks up what must be a butt plug—I've never seen one before, but I can guess at its use—and brings the tip to my anus. "This is your punishment, *mi amor*." He lifts my ankles—not high enough to pull my pelvis up off the bed this time—and nudges the bulbous tip of the slender stainless steel plug against my back hole.

My anus clenches, then, against my will, my body opens

for it. Carlos presses his advantage, easing the plug into me. The sensation is at once delicious and horrifying. I don't want to like it, but I do. Pleasure floods me as he works the cool metal phallus deeper. It's not too big, so while there's a sensation of stretching and filling, there's no discomfort, other than my embarrassment at having an object up my ass. He pushes it in until it seats, then rolls me to my belly and gives my ass a light slap.

I'm oddly disgruntled, not about having the plug in my ass, but now that it's in, I'm needy and flushed, wanting more. "Carlos?"

"*Madre de Dios*, *yes*, Sedona. Keep saying my name in that throaty voice of yours. It makes me want to jack off and come all over you."

A shocked little gust comes out of me—half laugh, half moan. Like before, I hike up my ass, offering an invitation for him to take what he's already claimed.

Fates know I want his cock again, just as badly as I'd wanted it the night he marked me.

He groans. "Are you offering me that pretty little pussy of yours, *ángel?*" He slips his fingers between my legs and strokes my slit.

My eyes roll back in my head. "Yes, Carlos." I hardly recognize my wanton moan.

Carlos dips into my juices and coats my inner lips with my own natural lubrication, circling my clit with maddening slowness. Then, at the same time, he starts to move the slender butt plug in and out of my ass.

I shout with surprise, the intensity of pleasure and need catapulting me into overdrive.

"C-Carlos!"

"You like that, doll?"

"Oh *fates*, please!"

"Please, what, beautiful?"

"Please don't stop. Please, faster—Carlos!" I try to convey my urgency by beating my feet on the bed, like a swimmer's kick, only from just the knees.

Somehow, despite my lack of sexual experience, I'm quite sure that the only thing better would be penetration of my pussy, too. As if Carlos reads my mind, he glides two fingers inside me, pumping them alternately with the plug.

My moans meld into one long, guttural cry. Probably everyone in the damn hotel can hear me, but whatever. It's Paris. "Carlos, Carlos, *please*," I beg. I seriously want to weep —I'm so wound up, need release so badly.

Carlos starts plunging his fingers and the plug at the same time, fast, and stars burst before my eyes. I feel like I'm hurtling into a dark tunnel on a roller coaster. It's Space Mountain all the way as everything in me shoots toward the finish line. It's more like a portal, than a line, though, because the second I pass through it, my body tightens and squeezes, wringing every last bit of pleasure out while my mind, my consciousness, soars. I coast into outer space, flung so far and so high I can't even remember my name. My age. My species.

And then I'm back. Panting into the bedspread as Carlos eases both his fingers and the plug from my body. He trails kisses across my lower back before he disappears to the bathroom to use the sink.

I'm boneless, incapable of moving from where I seem to have melted into the bed. When Carlos returns, he releases my wrists and gathers me up into his arms.

"Okay, *ángel*?"

Somehow I manage to nod. I try to make my lips move, to ask about his pleasure. I'd invite him to satisfy his earlier expressed fantasy of jacking off all over me, but no sound comes out.

Carlos presses a bottle of water to my lips and I drink.

"You're so beautiful," he murmurs in awe.

I don't need to be told—as an alpha female, it's something I've always known, but he doesn't seem to be saying it for my benefit. More like an observation he can't help but make.

"Are you hungry, *mi amor*? I bought some snacks for us, too."

I manage a weak nod. "When were you planning to feed me them?" I ask when he returns with a container of fresh strawberries, a baguette, and a jar of Nutella.

"I hadn't figured that part out yet." His rueful grin is humble and handsome and my remaining annoyance melts away. This is the male I remember from that cell in Mexico. The male I formed a bond with, whether I like it or not. He dips a strawberry into the Nutella and holds it up to my lips.

I take a bite, conscious of his gaze glued to my lips. A trickle of juice escapes my lips and Carlos lunges as my tongue flicks it away. He stops himself and swallows.

"Sedona. I-I have so many things I want to say, but none of them seem good enough. I'm sorry. I'll start with that. I'm sorry."

I look at him from under my lashes. "For what, exactly?"

"For what my pack did to you. I can never take it back. Never make it up to you. But the fates know I want to try."

I draw in a breath. I have to ask this question. I need to know how much of what happened in Mexico was biology —the full moon and two alphas locked together—and how much is real. "What about what you said back in the cell— that you weren't sorry it happened?"

Carlos clenches his jaw and busies himself with tearing

off a piece of bread and dipping it in the Nutella. He feeds it to me. "That's also true." His voice has the timber of a heavy confession, like he doesn't want to admit it, but can't lie.

I'm dismayed by how much lighter his admission makes me feel. How far have *I* fallen for this guy?

I'm loving the chocolate bread treat and I lift my chin to urge him to give me more. He does, immediately. I don't have any comparisons, but it's hard to imagine a more attentive lover.

"Sedona, I don't wish to force myself on you. The last thing I want is to make this all harder. But I'm also incapable of letting you go. I'm not saying that to scare you, I'm just trying to explain why I'm here, following you like a stray dog who smells meat."

My lips twitch at his comparison and I see relief seep across his expression.

"Let me serve as your escort on this trip. I know you came to forget me. To forget what happened. But I've been watching you for days, *mi amor,* and your melancholy hasn't lessened. Maybe you need a... *friend* to share your travels. I speak a little French and I'm very good at holding umbrellas and keeping the flocks of fans away from soon-to-be-famous artists when they stop to sketch things."

I arch a brow. "Friend, huh? Do you strip all of your friends naked and tie them to bedposts?" The minute I ask the question, I'm burning with jealousy. Has he done this before? He did seem rather expert at it. I want to poke the eyes out of every female he's been with.

His lips twitch. "You brought that on yourself, *blanca.* You should know better than to goad my wolf." He uses that authoritative tone that gets me wet.

"What's *blanca*—white?"

"Yes. So what do you say, *muñeca?* Will you let me stay? Be your companion?"

"That depends." I already know my answer is *yes*. The heaviness that's shrouded me since Mexico is lifting and European travel suddenly becomes as enticing as it felt when I first dreamed of coming here.

"Name your conditions, *mi amor*. I will respect them."

I love the honor and respect he shows me. "When I say I need space, you back off. I'm not accepting you as my mate."

He nods gravely. "Understood. I'm not asking for that."

Suddenly shy, I snatch up a strawberry and bite into it. I love the hungry expression that creeps over Carlos' face as he watches. I wonder if he's going to demand his own pleasure or deny himself to prove he'll behave. I'm tempted to confess to him that next time I'd love to try the butt plug and his cock, but I hold back.

He's not my mate, he's a companion. We still haven't discussed how doomed and impossible any future relationship would be, but the subject looms over us.

"Maybe we should go to Spain," I blurt to keep from jumping his bones.

"Why?"

"You speak the language. It might be more fun."

He leans his forehead against mine as he presses another strawberry between my lips. "That is a wonderful idea, *mi amor*. We'll go visit the haunts of Gaudí and Picasso. Dalí. Miró. Who else?"

I beam at him. Though I've been the princess of my father's pack my entire life, and many would call me spoiled, I always felt like no one knew me. Like I'm little more than an object or symbol. Carlos pays attention. He knows exactly what I like and I love the feeling of being truly *seen* for once. And the idea of visiting museums with him nearly makes me giddy.

I nestle my head against his shoulder, settling into the comfort he provides. For all my brave desires to do this trip alone, it's much nicer to have a partner. Especially one as capable and caring as Carlos.

 arlos

I SHOULD LEAVE Sedona's room before my throbbing cock makes me do something stupid and I erode the trust we just built. I breathe in her scent, which both tortures and relieves me at the same time. My sweet mate fell asleep on my shoulder—a pleasure I will work my ass off to earn for the rest of my life. Nothing felt better than providing for my mate—feeding her and sheltering her in my arms.

Well, nothing except bringing her to climax.

My wolf is still buffing his nails over that one. It was risky pushing her limits the way I did, but the payoff was huge. At Harvard, they taught us to analyze risk, figure out how to minimize it. It's suddenly clear me that playing it safe has never served me. It goes against my wolf nature, my alpha nature. And it's definitely the reason I have a shitstorm to deal with back at Monte Lobo.

Fuck the risks. My pack needs to be shaken up. The council needs their asses kicked and I'm the only one who can turn them on their heads. Changes need to be made, progress instilled.

Lying here with Sedona in my arms, everything is crystal clear. As if all I ever needed for actualization in life was to become Sedona's mate. If I'm man—well, wolf in our case—enough to be her mate, I've become the alpha who can properly lead his pack. And that may mean doing things differently than my father did them.

Whoa. Is it true that part of my reluctance to move forward stems from a desire not to out-do my sire? Mind-boggling and stupid, but there it is. I've been holding back out of honor for my father. If he didn't challenge the council, what made me think I should?

Unexpected grief seizes my chest. I feel disloyal for even thinking I can do better. But if I don't, I will never, ever win my mate. How can I hope to bring Sedona to a broken pack? What life could I give her?

I drop a light kiss on her forehead and ease her out of my arms and under the covers. I need to do something about my rock hard cock, or sleep will be an impossibility. If I were a better wolf, I'd leave her here and go down to my own room. But that's a fucking impossibility.

I will never leave Sedona of my own free will. Not unless she asks me to go.

I pad to the bathroom and shuck my clothes, climbing into the shower. Even with the water turned on cold, I can't get my cock to shut down.

Fuck it. I'll be better able to handle sleeping next to Sedona if I jerk off in here. I turn the temperature back to warm and fist my raging hard-on. All I have to do is think about Sedona, lying less than ten meters away. Naked.

I pump my hand over my cock, eyes already rolling back in my head. All I have to do is replay the moment I claimed her back in Monte Lobo, and I go off, coming against the shower wall, the heat of the water suddenly way too warm.

I change it to cold and rinse off.

Now, hopefully, I can lie next to her without danger of attacking her as she sleeps. I towel off and tug on my boxer briefs. But when I re-enter the bedroom, my cock lifts at the sight of her.

Hell. It's going to be a killer-long night.

~.~

Sedona

I DREAM CARLOS' hands are all over me, stroking my bare skin. He's growling something stern and domly that makes my toes curl.

No wait. Hold the phone. Those *are* Carlos' hands all over me. One glides over my hip, the other tangles in my hair.

I'm awake.

But I'm not even sure he's awake. His breath sounds slow, deep, and even like he's sleeping. I think his hands are roaming of their own accord.

"Carlos?"

There's a hitch in his breath and he stops stroking me. Then, judging by his resumed slow exhale, he slides back into slumber and begins the caress again.

Everywhere he touches me comes alive, heating and tingling. His hand strokes up my side, slides around to cup my breast. He squeezes it, rubbing his thumb over my nipple.

Seriously? The guy is so good in bed he can do it in his sleep? I should've followed up on my question about how many females he's entertained this way.

I squeeze my thighs together to alleviate the thrum of renewed desire building there. I blink at the bedside clock. It's four in the morning. If he keeps this up, I will never fall back to sleep.

I grasp his hand and slide it down between my legs.

Again, there's a pause in his breath before it relaxes back into an even cadence, but his fingers know just what to do. He strokes into me. I'm shocked at how wet I've already become.

I moan. Carlos growls.

Is he awake now? I can't tell.

"Carlos?"

The growls grow louder, his fingers quest deeper, parting my folds, penetrating me.

I choke out a cry and scissor my legs tight around his hand, hungry for full contact.

A snarl rips out of Carlos' throat and suddenly I'm pinned flat on my belly, his hand gripping my nape, his knees knocking my thighs wider.

My breath leaves me in a whoosh when he drops his weight onto me, thrusting his stiff cock in the notch between my legs.

I almost laugh. His cock is shielded from my entrance by his boxers, but he's not awake enough to realize. He growls in frustration, thrusting harder. If it weren't for the hand at my nape, I'd go flying into the headboard he's pounding so hard.

He figures out the problem and bares his cock and a half-second later he impales me with it. Fully. As in, to the hilt.

I cry out, not hurt, just shocked by the force and abandon of his thrusts. He pumps hard and fast, pistoning with powerful hip-snaps, slapping my ass with his loins. His growls fill the room, providing the bass to the soprano of my gasping cries.

I spread my legs wider, arch back to meet him, blinded with the deepest satisfaction.

Yes, *this*.

I never knew it could be so good. So right.

And sleep-fucking, no less.

Carlos' growls choke off and his body jerks to a stop. *"Puh."* He lets out a breath. He releases his grip on my nape and shoves the hair out of my face, but his hips start thrusting again, even faster than before.

I twist to look back, and he's staring down at me, his brows drawn together in a tight line.

"Sedona, oh *fates*—" He shouts his release, his voice echoing off the walls.

I swear I feel his hot cum fill me. I shove my hand down between my legs and rub my clit as I follow him to the finish.

He groans, still coming and rolls us toward our sides, reaching around to grasp both my breasts as he continues to thrust into me. His breath burns hot on my neck as he kneads my breasts, pinching my nipples.

I come again—an aftershock almost as good as the first one.

Carlos sucks and kisses my neck, groaning. I get the

feeling he's still coming back to consciousness. "Sedona, I'm so sorry. I didn't mean to—" The fingers I'm using on my clit scrape the base of his cock and he catches my wrist, pulling it up in front of our faces. "What is this?" His accent is so thick, so sexy. He takes my fingers into his mouth and sucks.

My pussy contracts as if he were sucking *down there*.

"*Mi amor,* you don't touch yourself when you're in bed with me. That's *my job*."

My heart, already racing from our interlude, picks up speed at the gravelly scolding.

He sucks my fingers again. "Mmm. You taste delicious, *ángel*. I'm sorry I didn't do my job well this time. I was, uh…"

"Asleep?" I giggle.

He drops his head into my neck and laughs. "I'm so sorry," he groans. "Did I hurt you? Are you all right?"

"I'm okay."

He lifts his head, peering into my face with an intensity that makes my pulse jump. "You sure? I didn't mean to do that to you, beautiful. I jacked off before I came to bed so I wouldn't force myself on you, and then I went and did it in my sleep. Without protection."

He looks so genuinely rueful.

"I would've stopped you if I didn't like it."

A look of wonder creeps over his face. "It was okay? You liked it?"

"I knew you were asleep. I was sort of amazed that you got so far with me without waking up. There ought to be an award for that or something."

He's still slowly pumping into me, even though we've both come and his cock is softening. He reaches between my legs and taps my clit lightly. "I deserve no award if you had to satisfy yourself, *mi amor*."

A second aftershock ripples through me. A little one this time, but no less pleasurable.

"Never again." He's pulling out the bossy tone once more. "I will be the one to give you pleasure, *ángel*. It's my duty. One I promise to take very seriously."

I want to giggle but he sounds dead serious. Like he's swearing a vow on his father's grave.

"O-okay." I don't know what else to say.

He lands an epic bite-suck-kiss on my neck. "Nobody else touches this," he growls, his voice low with warning. "Not even you."

I shiver at the possibility of more punishment at his hands if I disobey. The idea thrills me and I can hardly wait to try it out, but I play along. "Okay."

He nips the outer shell of my ear. "Good girl."

Warmth curls through me at his words and I settle back into his arms. Maybe I will be able to fall back to sleep.

11

*C*arlos

I CARRY coffee and croissants from the train snack cart to where Sedona sketches on her pad. The trip from Paris to Barcelona takes six and a half hours by speed train and I've done everything I can think of to make things easy and enjoyable for Sedona. I bought us comfort class tickets and paid for three seats instead of two so we wouldn't have to sit with anyone else. I set up her phone to charge in the outlet between our seats and offered her my iPod and earbuds for music.

I love to watch her work, so absorbed in her sketch of a fairy alight a flower.

She barely looks up as I set the food down on my tray, but I don't take offense. I don't want to intrude on her time, I'm just grateful she's allowed me to take care of her.

I pull my phone out and call Monte Lobo. It's Sunday,

and it was my habit when away to call my mother on Sundays. Of course, she doesn't have her own phone, since technology is banned for all but the council and alpha.

I call Don Santiago, who acts as a sort of gatekeeper for the pack. Almost all transmissions go through him. I don't like Don Santiago—I don't like any of the council members —but he's probably the most capable. Like me, he went to university. He has an advanced degree, even worked for a time in a genetics lab in Mexico City. He's been out in the world enough to understand how things work, including technology and how best to use it. He was the one responsible for getting the mountain wired for Wi-Fi despite the rest of the council's dire predictions that connecting us to the world would lead to our destruction.

Don Santiago answers on the second ring. "Carlos." He always goes for this hearty, grandfatherly tone with me.

"Hello, Don Santiago," I say in Spanish. "How are things?" It's the same conversation we had every week I was away in college.

"All is well here, *mijo*." He calls me *my son*, which always makes me bristle.

I don't let it slide this time. "Carlos. Or Don Carlos. Not son." I'm pleased I can say it coolly with nary a growl.

"Of course, I'm sorry Don Carlos," Don Santiago smooths. "It's just that I've known you since you were a baby."

"And now I'm alpha."

"Yes, of course. No one challenges that."

For some reason his words make the hairs on my arms stand up. He said it too quickly, too easily. As if I really do need to worry that there will be a challenge. I store that away to chew on later.

"Did you find your female, Carlos?"

I stifle a growl again. I don't like anyone talking about my female, especially not any of the fucking council members. "I found her."

"And?"

This time I do rumble. "I am taking her to Barcelona. A honeymoon of sorts." I glance guiltily at Sedona, even though she doesn't speak Spanish. I'm not sure she would appreciate my calling this a honeymoon, since she hasn't agreed to be my mate, but I'm just saying the thing Santiago wants to hear. To get him off my fucking back. "Is my mother available?" I ask impatiently.

"I'm walking to her quarters now. Let's see if she's coherent today."

I gnash my teeth, even though it's not Don Santiago's fault whether she's coherent or not. In fact, I used to depend on Don Santiago to be the one who would give it to me straight about my mother. But after Maria Jose's suggestion I have someone else look at her, a seed of doubt has crept in. Does Don Santiago have her best interest at heart? What if they're not giving her the best care possible? What if I should have sought to return her to her own family after my father died?

It's not too late—I can look into it when I return. Yet another issue to address.

I hear Don Santiago's voice and my mother's in response, then she comes on the line. "Carlos?"

"Hello, *Mamá*. How's it going?"

"Carlos? Where are you?"

"I'm in Barcelona, *Mamá,* with the girl I told you about."

"In Barcelona?" She sounds confused. Nothing new there.

"Yes, with my female."

My mom gives a loud gasp, and a spike of fear rushes

through me before she proclaims, "How wonderful! Carlos has a mate."

"Are you crying, *Mamá?*"

"I'm just so happy for you, Carlos. When are you going to bring her home?"

"I'm not sure." A fact which kills me. "Soon, I hope." Not a lie—I can always hope.

"Grandpups. I want grandpups, Carlos."

A rush of longing goes through me so strongly I have to close my eyes. *Sedona, pregnant with my pup.* My entire life would be worth living if that were the case. And I would damn well make sure their life was perfect.

I clear my throat. "I want that, too, *Mamá.*"

Sedona is looking over at me with curiosity, taking her ear buds out of her ears.

"Listen, *Mamá,* I have to go. I'll call you next week. Take care of yourself."

"I love you, Carlitos, *mijo.* Bring the she-wolf back here. I want to meet her."

"Yes, *Mamá.* I love you, too. *Ciao.*"

I end the call and turn to Sedona and shrug. "My mother."

"Was she—" Sedona seems to struggle for the words. I appreciate her sensitivity.

"She was mostly coherent. I told her about you." I fidget with the croissants, pulling one out of the paper sleeve to offer it to her.

"What did you say?"

"Well, I told her about you the morning you left, but she'd forgotten. I told her I was here with you now. She cried."

Sedona's watching me too intently for comfort. I break off a piece of croissant and pop it between her lips.

"I am capable of feeding myself, you know."

"I like to feed you."

She smiles as she chews. "I know you do. So, why did she cry?"

"She's happy for me. I didn't tell her any of the, uh, history. Only that I'm here with my female—a female," I amend.

The sadness I saw on Sedona's face all last week creeps back over and I want to shoot myself for making her remember. There's so much ugliness in our past—because of the council. I don't want to bring it up, but I know we have to face it at some point. I take a deep breath.

"Listen. We'll figure it out. I know it's a lot to overcome—what we've been through, our differences, where we live. But give us a chance, Sedona."

"I don't know, Carlos. We live in different worlds."

"We're two educated, intelligent wolves. We can make it work."

Her brow wrinkles, gaze going far away.

I grab her hand to bring her back. "I've been thinking of the way things are in Monte Lobo. I always planned to change things as soon as I became alpha. I've only been back a few weeks, and it hasn't been as easy as I expected, but I promise things will be different.

"Sedona, first of all, I want you to know I tried to avenge your kidnapping, but someone got there first."

"Garrett. My brother."

I nod.

"Second, I want to say, what the council did to you—to us—was wrong. When I get back, I'll be turning things upside down. There are many good wolves in the pack, and they deserve better." Something in me shifts as I speak. I make the vow in my heart as I tell Sedona, "I'm going to root out corruption and carry the pack out of the Dark Ages. I will be the alpha they need."

Sedona studies my face. I stay very still, wondering what she sees in me.

"Okay." Something relaxes in her. "I'm glad."

"Thank you." I'm glad she listened. I can't tell if I won her trust, though.

"One thing's for sure," she says. "Your council..." She shakes her head. "You can't trust them. Not after what they did."

"I know. After my father died, they ran the show. I was too young to lead and there was no other clear alpha. They've taken way too much power. It will take a while to undo the damage they have done."

"So you will return to Mexico?" she asks, and my heart seizes. This is the topic I've been avoiding.

I take a deep breath. "I want to say no. See there's this beautiful female wolf who captivates me..."

Sedona smiles.

"But she wouldn't respect me if I abandoned my duties."

"No, she wouldn't."

"But I had to see her again. Even just for a few days. Monte Lobo is so oppressive, but the sight of her reminds me of what I'm fighting for. I'm hoping she will enjoy the next few days with me. We can pretend to be tourists who just met and travel together on a whim."

She raises a brow.

"It's a long shot, but I'm hoping she'll understand. I need this. Even if only for a few days."

"I understand," she says softly, a shadow passing over her face.

"Hey," I cup her cheek. "We don't have to decide anything. Let's just focus on enjoying Spain together."

"Okay."

A weight lifts off my chest. I have no answers for the future, but my wolf is happy to dwell in the now, basking in the presence of his chosen mate.

I pop another bite of croissant in her mouth. "May I see your drawing?"

She reaches for the pad, then hesitates, shooting me an inscrutable look.

"Please?"

I hold my breath as she slowly passes it to me, hoping I say the right things. The fairy is adorable—huge, wide-set eyes, a bow-tie mouth and red pigtails. Dainty long lines make up her body to give the impression of movement, like she's about to flit off to the next flower. She has her hands clasped behind her back, like Degas' *Little Dancer,* but so much cuter. There's a joyful, impish quality—I don't know enough about art to understand how Sedona produced it, but it's there.

"It's... *perfect.* You have a real talent, Sedona."

"Oh please." She tries to snatch it back, but I hold it out of her reach. "It's nothing. Cartoon-y stuff."

"That's not nothing. It's beautiful. It's bewitching. And most importantly, it's what you want to create." I can't help but think of monetizing her art—it was pounded into me at Harvard. "These would make perfect greeting cards. Or children's books. Even t-shirts."

She nibbles her lip, but I see a spark of hope in her eyes and I want to fist-pump. I said the right thing. "I-I don't really know. I'm not good with marketing or selling. I just like to create."

"Then let me sell them for you. I'll act as your agent. Or business-manager—whatever artists have." I grin.

"That'd be cool." She says it like she believes it won't

happen, which pisses me off. It makes me even more determined to prove to her how hard I'd work for her happiness.

I flip a page back and she tries to snatch it away. I twist to hold it out of her reach, where I can see it.

It's me—my wolf, in loving detail. She has my coloring right, my eyes. She remembered everything, even though she's only seen him once.

"Sedona." I turn back to her, eyes wide with awe. "You drew *me*."

Her cheeks are pink. She shrugs like it's nothing. "Why wouldn't I?"

"May I have it?"

"No." She reaches for it and this time I reluctantly let her have it.

Disappointment lances through me. "Why not?"

"I want to keep it," she mumbles.

My nose-diving confidence takes a sharp turn. She wants to keep it. The drawing of *me*. I want to read so much into this, but I know that's not wise. She hasn't admitted any feelings for me yet.

"I want one of you, then," I demand.

She gives a snort. "I don't draw myself." Her cheeks turn an enchanting shade of pink.

"Try."

She rolls her eyes, but a smile plays around her mouth. "I'll think about it."

I settle back in my seat and sip the coffee, laying one hand on her leg. Touching her grounds me, eases my anxiety even as it revs the engines of lust always burning in her presence.

It feels easy and comfortable with her and I hardly dare think it, but I'm starting to believe we can find a way to make things work.

I don't know how yet, but I know I want to try.

~.~

COUNCIL ELDER

I SETTLE into my first class seat on the plane to Europe and pull out my laptop. I have a great many lab results to review from the tests run in Mexico City. Fortunately, they were at a lab, not the warehouse. I didn't chance stopping there, in case it's being watched. Not by Federales—they can be paid off. But by shifters. Word is a wolf who wasn't part of the American party got free when they did and his pack is now on the hunt.

Good luck to them. I've done an excellent job staying behind the scenes. It's easy when you're willing to pay top dollar for services rendered.

I scan the results, studying the genetic markers of the American she-wolf, as well as those of her pack mates. All healthy. Too bad I didn't have time to extract eggs and semen to initiate *in vitro* fertilization.

All the more reason Carlos needs to get his female pregnant on this trip, if the deed is not already done.

Barcelona.

Carlos couldn't have made my job any easier. I have a warehouse there, with two she-wolves, one jaguar, and two bears in captivity there, all transported in from Siberia.

I could have them transported to Mexico, but Carlos

made the decision easy for me. I'll kill two birds with one stone.

If Carlos doesn't cooperate, I'll imprison him and his little American, and breed them another way. Better than killing him, like his father. What a waste.

I send a message to Aleix, one of the traffickers. *There are two new wolves in your city. Find them, watch them, but don't touch them—they are under my protection.*

~.~

SEDONA

CARLOS HOLDS my hand as we walk up Las Ramblas, the open air pedestrian mall in Barcelona. I try not to read too much into it—whether I should let him hold my hand, or the message it sends. He's already sleeping in my room, waking me up at night to fuck my brains out. Probably hand-holding shouldn't be a hard limit.

The street is packed with tourists and vendors and I have to admit, I enjoy the way Carlos embodies safety and protection.

I stop to check out a street performer pretending to be statue for a moment, then Carlos leads me to the Miró mosaic set in the sidewalk where tourists tramp right over it, never knowing it's a famous work of art.

I check out a collection of leather bags at one vendor, and Carlos pulls his wallet out, as he has every time I've stopped. He's so eager to buy me anything my heart desires.

Too bad I'm not some starving artist, or he could work that angle to bind me to him.

That was a weird thought.

It's just that he's so actively wooing me. He's proving he can provide, taking care of my every need. It's sweet as hell, but also unnerves me if I think about it too hard. I feel like I'm on a reality television show where I have a limited amount of time to get to know bachelor number one and decide if he's the guy I'm going to spend the rest of my life with.

Um, no.

Carlos and I have chemistry, no doubt about that. But I can't decide how much of the rest of it is real. Is he here wooing me because his biology forces him to? His wolf won't let me go now that he's marked me?

Isn't there some better girl for him? Someone from his own culture, who speaks the language and doesn't mind the crazy council?

But even as I think that, I hate this imagined mate. She'd be all wrong for him, I just know.

I set down the leather bag I'm examining.

"Do you want one?" Carlos asks.

I shake my head. "No thanks, money bags."

He lifts a brow. "Money bags?"

"Are you trying to show what a good provider you are?"

He chuckles. "I'm old-fashioned. Maybe so."

"What is your financial situation, anyway?" I ask, then immediately kick myself because now I sound like the bachelorette interviewing her prospect.

"My pack has wealth. Generally, it all goes to the hacienda and the rest are left with nothing."

He says this matter-of-factly, but I know it's not something he's accepted, or he wouldn't call it to my attention.

"So are you going to redistribute the wealth?"

"It's not quite so easy. I want to divert the money to infrastructure—plumbing and electricity, better housing. But I think we could also change the way we do business to increase profits. I've been examining the books and we should be making more. Much more."

"Do you think someone's stealing it?"

He meets my eye. "To be honest? Yes."

I squeeze his hand. "Well, I'm sure you'll figure out who and take care of it. That's why you're there, right?"

He loops an arm around my waist and twirls me into him, my breasts pressing up against his ribs. "Everything seems doable when I'm with you."

My heart stutters and I melt into him, lifting my face for a kiss.

He ghosts his lips over mine. "You give me reason," he murmurs.

Part of me wants to draw away, to deny him *me* as his reason. I'm not ready for that commitment. But fireworks are going off in my chest and I'm smiling up at him like a goofball.

His kiss is warm and tender, infused with something deeper than passion.

It scares the crap out of me.

~.~

Carlos

. . .

I step out of the shower after a day spent touring the Gaudí House Museum with Sedona. I swear she makes everything magical. Gaudí's architecture is impressive, no doubt, but seeing it through her eyes made it all the more glorious.

With a towel wrapped around my waist, I walk out of the bathroom into our hotel room and find Sedona. In the red dress.

"Oh no, *muñeca*. You're not wearing that out," I say with complete authority. I have to prevent this catastrophe, or I will be ripping out the eyes of every male who sees her tonight.

Not to mention the additional problem of us not making it to dinner because I now want to throw her up against the wall and ball her brains out.

"Dress off. You can't wear that." Bad move on my part, but I can't stop the dictate from flying out of my mouth.

She throws her hands on her hips. "Fuck. You. I'll wear whatever I damn well please."

Okay, yeah. I totally fucked up on that one.

I stalk toward her, a hunter after his prey. I shove my wolf down before speaking this time. "Forgive me, *mi amor*. I didn't mean it like that." My hands reach for her hips and I slide the fabric up to reveal more thigh. "I just meant if you wear that, the only thing I'll be eating tonight will be you."

One of those beautiful smiles lights up her face. "I'm counting on that."

I groan. "But you're starving. You already said so—twice —before we got back here to shower and change."

"You'll have to contain yourself until after dinner." She covers my palms with hers to stay them.

"Impossible."

She shrugs. "Then I'll go alone."

"The hell you will," I growl. This time I can't help but

crowd her back against the wall and trap her between my arms. "Take off. The dress."

Her eyes dilate. The corners of her lips kick up. "No." I hear the challenge in her voice. It's the same one that tells me to chase when she runs.

But somewhere, somehow, I also remember that she's hungry. It's my duty to provide for my female. So I'll have to make this quick. I spin her around to face the wall and fist the fabric of her skirt in back to pull it up.

She's wearing miniscule panties—tiny, G-string satin threads with a scrap of fabric between her legs.

I rip them off her, unable to contain myself enough to take them off gently. "Who are those for?" I growl, insanely jealous because she had those panties with her, she brought them to Paris, before she knew I'd join her.

"Easy, big guy," she soothes. "They're for you. Only for you. Like this pussy." She reaches between her legs and touches herself.

Oh no she didn't.

I snake an arm around her waist to hold her in place and spank her lush ass, my hand falling fast and hard. My other hand slides down her belly to cup her mons. She's dripping wet. I press one finger into her wet heat, use it to spread moisture up to her clit. She closes her fingers over mine, rocks down for more attention down there.

I suck my breath in over my teeth and stop spanking, squeezing and massaging her heated curves as I stroke her wet pussy. "Turn around." My voice is three octaves lower than usual, more beast than man.

She turns and I shake the towel off my waist. When she slides a leg up around my waist, I scoop my forearm under her ass, lifting her to meet my throbbing member.

And then I'm in her. Exactly where I've wanted to be all day. Where I needed to be last night, and the night before.

I thrust in and up, pushing her shoulders against the wall, but holding her hips out to meet mine. She's a disheveled goddess, dress tangled up around her waist, hair sprawled out on the wall. I fuck her hard and deep, relentless.

"I wanted to give it to you slow tonight, baby. Take my time with you. But no, you had to wear *that* dress," I growl as I bang into her.

She clutches my shoulders, nails scoring my flesh, marking me as I've marked her. "Carlos," she chokes. The desperation is there already, she needs to come.

Good thing, because longevity isn't in the cards for me at the moment.

"Take it," I growl. "Take it deep, *muñeca*. You asked for this."

As usual, my female is excited by my dirty talk. She shatters, inner thighs squeezing my waist, pussy clenching and releasing as her last cry hangs, seemingly suspended in the air between us because she's stopped breathing.

I slam into her three more times and plunge deep for my finish.

Sedona's chest moves again, and she slides her hands around, digs her nails deep into my back, closes her eyes.

I claim her mouth, slanting my lips over hers, licking and sucking until I stop coming. Then I freeze. "I forgot a condom again." I'd worn one last night, but the night before, when I sleep-fucked her, I hadn't worn one, and now I did it again. As horrible as it sounds, I subconsciously must want her to get pregnant, to bind her to me.

"It's okay." She tucks her face into my neck, still recovering her breath. "You can't get me pregnant."

Relief pours through me. Well, mostly relief. Maybe with ten percent disappointment. She must be on the pill. Strange, but I hadn't smelled it the way I can smell it on a human female.

Her stomach rumbles.

"Baby, you're hungry," I chide. I ease out of her and lower her feet to the floor. "Let's go get some dinner."

She stands still and I look up from where I'd bent to pick up my towel.

"Sedona. Fuck." I stalk back to her, wrapping the towel around my waist. "Did I hurt you? I was way too rough. I'm sorry, *ángel*."

She reaches for me, which nearly floors me with relief. Wraps her arms around my neck and lets me hold her. "I like it when you're rough," she murmurs against my ear. Her body is trembling, though, and I feel like the biggest ass for fucking her and then dropping her to the floor while I wipe off my dick.

I hold her, stroking her back, burying my face in her thick glossy hair. I'm replaying the scene, trying to figure out if something went wrong, or if she just needs a moment of aftercare when she says, "You owe me a pair of panties, though."

I bark a laugh.

"And I'm still wearing this dress out."

I groan. "Okay, *muñeca*, wear the dress. But you'll be held responsible for all the men whose faces meet my knuckles when they ogle you."

She lets go of me and I reluctantly step back. "You'll behave." She sounds like she believes it, which makes me vow to meet her expectations. Even if it fucking kills me.

~.~

SEDONA

I DIDN'T LIE. Not exactly.

He can't get me pregnant because I already am.

My insides swim around with the misdirection and all the issues I've avoided examining come slamming back into me.

It won't be long before he scents the change in hormones on me. Before my body starts to change to accommodate the new life within me. Our pup.

What will it mean to him?

I don't even know what it means to me.

Fates, this entire trip to Europe wasn't to heal, it was a last ditch effort to spread my wings before I'm saddled with a child. I've been pretending that child doesn't exist, pretending none of my problems exist while I get my rah-rahs out seeing famous art and getting sexed against the wall by a libidinous werewolf.

But I'm going to have to face the music soon. Either I lose Carlos soon and try to keep this pregnancy from him or we stick together and he'll find out on his own in the next week or two.

Then what?

If he's already gone overboard to protect me on this trip, what do I think he'll do when he knows I'm carrying his pup? Do I really believe he'll ever leave my side?

What did Garrett say? *It would take an entire pack to keep him away.*

I slip on a new pair of panties and smooth the skirt of the dress back down as Carlos gets dressed.

He's looking over at me like he knows something's going on in my head and it worries him. He pays attention, I'll give him that. Moments like these I wish he'd pay a little less attention.

No, that's not true.

Carlos escorts me out and we walk down to Las Ramblas again and find an open-air restaurant where we can watch all the activity on the tree-lined street.

I'm sore and used in all the right places, but I know it will fade within the next hour, so I savor every twinge and pulse.

Carlos orders a bottle of wine after consulting me on my preferences. When it comes, I take a sip, but even if I'd wanted to drink alcohol, I can't. My body totally refuses it. I can barely choke down one sip.

After we order our food, Carlos asks, "What's going on in that beautiful mind of yours, Sedona? You're too quiet."

I shake my head. "Nothing. Just trying not to think about what comes next with us."

His expression turns grave. He stares a hole through me and I can't breathe. "Now I'm trying not to ask you what you're trying not to think about."

I give a short laugh, grateful for his ability to be so real with me. For it to be this easy to talk about something so hard.

The waiter brings our food and I tuck in, devouring my meal like I haven't eaten in a week. I hope this isn't the start of pregnancy cravings, because I don't want to spend the next nine months eating everything in sight.

Ugh. And now I'm thinking about the pregnancy again. Not that I ever stopped.

I look out onto the pedestrian thoroughfare at a pair of musicians who just started up and Carlos follows my line of sight. He chokes on his wine and I look over, amused.

"Everything okay over there?"

He dabs his lips with his napkin. "Yes. I'm going to use the restroom, *muñeca*. I'll be back in just a moment."

It takes about thirty seconds for it to sink into my brain that he didn't head in the direction of the restrooms, he headed toward the exit.

My instincts roar to life, hairs standing up at the back of my neck, vision tunneling like I need to shift and run. But what is the danger? I look around, and catch sight of Carlos out on La Rambla, talking with...

Oh fuck no.

It's one of the council members. I'd remember that old son-of-a-bitch anywhere. He's one of the two males who met the traffickers at the gate.

I throw some Euros on the table and get up, marching out of the restaurant. I'm so focused on Carlos and the council member, I don't see a group of young men coming until they bump into me. Something pricks my arm and I nearly lose my balance, but one of them catches me. They are laughing and talking in Spanish—no, not Spanish—Catalan, the first language in Barcelona. One of them holds my elbow and says something friendly to me, but I shake them off, still barreling toward Carlos.

When I go to wipe away the stinging on my arm, my hand comes away bloody.

It's nothing, but it adds fuel to my fury and sense of violation. A fury which Carlos is about to get the full brunt of.

~.~

CARLOS

DON SANTIAGO IS HERE in Barcelona.

I'm ready to pound him into the ground. I don't know what his game is, but I intend to find out. Now.

If we weren't in a public place, I would already have his throat in my hand.

"Relax, *mijo*—Don Carlos—I'm not *spying* on you, as you say. I had business to attend to here and I thought it would be a good time for a visit."

"Bullshit."

Don Santiago hasn't wiped his indulgently amused expression off his face yet and I'm about ready to do so with my fist. "*Bueno.* You're right. The council has a stake in how you're doing here with your female. I came to see if I could be of service."

"*Of service?*" It takes all my effort not to shout the words. "What, are you going to send a mango and wine to our hotel room? Help get us in the mood?"

Don Santiago folds his arms over his chest. "Do I need to?"

I clench my fists so hard my nails dig into my palms.

"Is she pregnant yet?"

Don Santiago looks over my shoulder at the same moment I catch Sedona's scent.

Carajo!

I whirl, but it's too late. She heard.

Her face is pale as snow, but fury blazes in her eyes.

"Sedona—this isn't what you think."

She's already turned away from me, walking with purposeful strides in the direction of our hotel.

"Sedona—wait! Let me explain." I chase after her. I stop myself just before I reach for her, because I'm sure she will deck me if I lay a hand on her. I opt for matching her stride, instead. "I don't know why he's here. I didn't know he was coming. *Listen to me.*"

"No." She stops and throws a hand out against my chest, halting me, too. "I don't have to listen to you. In fact, I can't. I won't. I heard what he wants. Whether you claim to be innocent in your council's dirty little plan or not, you're a part of it. And that means I'm out." She starts walking again.

"Fuck!" I can't help cursing out loud before I pick up my pace beside her. "That's not what—"

Except it is. She nailed it. I can't argue with her take on what's going down.

"Sedona, I'm not here to get you pregnant. I don't see you as prize. I came because I couldn't stay away. I wanted to honor your request for space, but... I just *couldn't.*"

"Well you're going to have to," she snaps. "Because I'm done."

She's done with me.

Her words drive a spike straight through my gut.

I slow my steps, let her advance without me. I'm not going to convince her to be with me by continuing to disrespect her wishes.

She doesn't even glance back, still marching on toward the hotel. My chest feels like it's been crushed by a hundred pound weight. I sag against the side of a building, hardly able to drag breath into my lungs.

She's right. Our problems are insurmountable. She'll never be able to forget what the council did to her and I am part of that horror. How could I even have hoped to bring her back with me?

The idea is ludicrous. It would only ruin her, like Monte Lobo ruined my mother. All her light would go out, she'd die a little more every day until she was either crazy, like my mother, or nothing but a shell.

Maybe if I had another plan to offer her. A different pack, another option. Maybe if I was willing to leave my pack, live with hers. But I can't abandon mine. My absence is part of the reason everything's fucked there. The pack needs me.

No, if I care about Sedona—truly care—and I do, then the only right thing is let her walk away.

Even if it means my chest caves in from the weight on it.

~.~

Sedona

I sense the second Carlos drops back and lets me go.

I know I should consider it a gift, but it wounds me as much as his deception. I march forward toward the hotel, refusing to look back. I don't want to see his expression. Don't want to think about what he's feeling now.

Is she pregnant yet?

I can't fucking believe his council is here monitoring us still. Have they been watching everything? Our meeting in Tucson? Paris? I hate them. I really do. I hate them with a bitterness that runs so deep I might drown in it.

But no. This anger is the other side of the coin to being a victim. Which I'd decided not to be.

They don't control me. They're not going to shape my life or my future. They're especially not going to shape my pup's future.

I run up to our hotel room and throw my things in my suitcase. I'm going home. Maybe I'm running scared. Yeah, I am running scared. But I have more than my own safety to consider. I have the safety of my baby.

And seeing that council member here shook me up. Badly. Every hair on my arms stands up as I replay the scene. He was watching us.

I may have thought I escaped when I left Mexico, but I didn't. They're still here with me.

And they still believe I'm their breeder.

Tears blur my vision as I grab my suitcase and head out of the hotel room. I half expect Carlos to be standing outside the room, or downstairs in the lobby, or on the side-walk outside the hotel, but he's not. No one stops me when I hail a cab and ask for the airport.

I know there's a chance I won't find any flights out at this time of night, but I don't give a crap. Every cell in my body screams for me to get out of here, fast. I need to get back to my family. To my pack, who will protect me.

Carlos can't be trusted. I don't even know if I can believe anything he said, anything that happened between us. It could have all been a fabrication to get me pregnant.

I'm glad now I didn't tell him.

There's a chance he's just as evil as his council.

That thought hurts worse than any other. To believe Carlos duped me or played me, that he never cared, leaves me clutching my chest to rid the searing pain.

I want to believe his feelings were real. But it's not

enough. He may have a biological need to be near me and protect me because he's marked me, but it doesn't mean he *loves* me. It doesn't mean we're well-suited as mates.

I was vulnerable and I read too much into his attention but I need to harden myself now.

For my pup's sake.

~.~

COUNCIL ELDER

I SNAP OPEN the tiny vial of blood and inhale deeply.

Good. The American is pregnant. I had a few humans bump into her and get a blood sample. It isn't enough for a lab test, but I can tell by the scent.

Carlos is no longer needed. If he gives us any more trouble, we'll kill him off faster than he can whine *don't call me mijo*.

And now I have his female's DNA too. Perfect for my gene manipulation tests. Soon I'll have harvested samples from every specimen of shifter on Earth. Enough to build a comprehensive DNA workup and determine the factors that improve or limit the ability to shift, to heal, to reproduce.

What happened in my pack will never have to happen again, because I'll be able to manipulate genes to create super-wolves, splicing in not only the best traits from werewolves, but also from other shifters.

I walk through the warehouse with a clipboard and match each species with their blood sample data. A tiger throws itself against the metal bars, snarling at me as I stand in front of him.

"This one is beautiful. Where did you find him?" I ask Aleix.

"Bought him from an Iranian, but he comes from Turkey."

"A Caspian tiger? Very rare find. The animal counterpart is extinct. Good work. I'll pay a hefty bonus for this one."

"I'm counting on it." Aleix folds his arms across his chest. He wants me to pay up now. I've made him and his brother Ferran extremely wealthy over the past ten years. They don't participate in any of the hunting of shifters— only the purchasing and storage, the blood draws and lab workups. Aleix is the businessman, Ferran is the bioscientist.

They wouldn't be in for any of this, except I've promised to cure their sister of the genetic disease causing her to slowly waste away. The truth is, I could've cured her years ago, but I know as soon as I do, Aleix and Ferran will fold and they're too valuable to me. Better to keep them working, seeking answers.

The Harvester needs his henchmen.

12

C *arlos*

THIRTY-FIVE HOURS since Sedona left me.

Every minute, every hour, feels like an eternity. Every breath takes effort to pull in. Every heartbeat pangs my chest.

I hire a car to drive me from *el D.F.* to Monte Lobo. I always feel heavy when I return to my home, but this time the weight of it makes it hard for me to even move. This must be what it feels like to be one hundred years old, the ache of every year pressing on your bones. Except in my case, it's the weight of every minute away from Sedona.

Every minute with my mind turning over our last moment together. I hate that she thinks I might be a part of the council's idiotic obsession with my future offspring. I hate knowing Don Santiago triggered the trauma of her ordeal again.

But now I know with complete certainty—it's impossible for us to be together. I could never bring her back here. All she would remember is the evil done to her.

A growl starts up in my throat. I should've killed every member of the council the moment they set us free. Am I such a coward to turn away from murder?

I scrub my face, but it does nothing to clear the cobwebs hanging over my eyes. If only I could find my way out of this legacy of gloom.

Juanito runs out to meet me, his childish face, sometimes appearing so old with the burdens he carries, shines. "Don Carlos!" He skids to a stop, reaches enthusiastically for my suitcase. I let him take it, not because he's a servant and I think it's his job, but because denying him would cause disappointment.

I ruffle his hair. "What's new, my friend?"

The boy shrugs. "Nothing. Did you bring your female back? They said you would."

The hole in my chest blows open even wider. "No. She can't return here. She would never forgive the council for taking her prisoner."

Juanito looks up at me. "Do you?"

"No." I don't. And I should really clean house—throw them all out at the very least. But I don't know if I have any allies here, apart from my nine-year-old friend.

Juanito nods, like he expected that answer. "Me neither." He pushes open my bedroom door and leaves the suitcase.

I sigh and go to see my mother. The sooner I get that visit over with, the sooner I can get out and walk the land. Hope the answers somehow come to me.

Tomorrow, heads will roll. Even if one of them ends up being my own.

~.~

Sedona

IT WAS EASIER to get a flight to Phoenix than Tucson, so that's where I go, calling my mom to pick me up from the airport.

The moment I see her, I'm like a child again. I burst into tears and throw myself into her arms while she lets out a stream of mother babble. "Fates, Sedona, I've been so worried—are you all right?—are you hurt?—what did they do to you?—tell me everything."

I pull away and dash at my tears with the back of my hand. "I'm marked and pregnant. I thought I might be in love, but it's not going to work out. So I'm home."

"For good?" My mom can't hide her joy. Of course she would love to have a grandpup around to spoil.

"I don't know, mom." The tears start again. "I don't know what to do."

She bustles me out to the car, where my dad's waiting by the curb. He gets out and gives me a bear hug, and for once, says nothing. Maybe I hurt him by going with Garrett after the Mexico thing.

No, that's stupid. My dad doesn't get hurt. He's probably trying to give me space. First time for everything.

He takes my suitcase and throws it in the trunk.

"Sedona's pregnant," my mom whispers as I climb in the back seat. Great.

My dad climbs in and pulls into traffic. "You okay, baby?"

I swallow and nod. "Yeah."

"Are they after you?"

A chill runs through me. Are they? Did they send Carlos to bring me back and when he failed, went themselves? Or again, is Carlos really the mastermind behind the Breed Sedona Project?

No. I know in my bones he isn't. He can't be. My instincts aren't that off.

"I don't know, Daddy," I admit. "Maybe. Or they will be when they find out about the pup."

"You'll stay here, then. Where I can protect you."

I bristle even though I knew that's what he'd say, and I truly need his protection. It's just that he doesn't ask, he orders.

"Garrett can protect me," I say stubbornly, even though I don't want to return to Tucson. Not now, anyway. There's nothing for me there.

But there's nothing for me here, either.

And there wasn't much for me in Europe until Carlos showed up.

Hell. Is this what it's like to have your heart broken? Life without your lover is nothing but shit?

Will this feeling of loss and loneliness ever go away? Can I find meaning again? Maybe with our child. Fates, I hope I can kick this overwhelming sadness before he or she comes.

My dad gives a non-committal snort. I seriously hope he's not insinuating the reason I was kidnapped was because Garrett didn't do a good enough job. He starts the car and lurches out into traffic. "We've been looking into things. Your brother killed the men who kidnapped you, but they weren't the wolves in charge. There's someone bigger. No one knows his identity, but he's called The Harvester. He buys wolves—other shifters too."

"What does he do with them?" My voice is hoarse.

"It's unclear. None of The Disappeared have returned, except for you."

Something tickles my consciousness, my instincts gunning, and I rub a spot on my arm. I remember the blood there after I bumped into the group of humans on Las Ramblas. I grip my arm and examine the area. There's nothing there. Why would that memory surface now?

My blood. Had someone wanted my blood? Had that crowd of jostling humans been an excuse to draw a sample of blood from me? But why?

Duh. To see if I'm pregnant. But was that the council or the Harvester? Probably the council.

"I think they *are* after me, Daddy." My voice sounds so hoarse I don't recognize it.

"Who? Your mate or his pack? Or both?"

"I-I don't know. His pack, I think." Sickness twists in my belly. I put a hand over my abdomen, sending a secret message of safety to my baby.

I won't let them have you.

"There's a shifter up in Flagstaff who we think might be from their pack. Old she-wolf. I've asked for a meeting."

"What did she say?"

"I'm waiting to hear. I contacted their alpha. Hopefully he'll get back to me today and I can drive up to talk to her."

"I want to go, too," I say.

My father hesitates, meeting my eyes in the rear view mirror. He gives a single nod.

I'm surprised—I'm used to him keeping me out of the fray. Things are changing.

~.~

Carlos

I storm into Don Jose's office. I've been back for a day and it's time to make some changes around here. "According to my calculations, we pull fifty thousand ounces of silver out of that mine each year and yet we're only selling thirty. Where is the rest of it going?"

Surprise flits over Don Jose's face, but he quickly masks it. "We're selling everything we pull out. What are you insinuating? That someone is stealing half our silver? Impossible." He scoffs and waves his hand, like he wants to shoo me away.

"Come now, Carlos. You've been in a temper since you returned without your female. I know you blame Don Santiago and the rest of us for that failing, but now you're getting paranoid."

I ignore the dig and slap the old ledgers on the desk. "Here are the reports from each mine on their production output." I point at several columns of numbers. "These don't match the reports turned in by Guillermo's team down at the mine." I set a dirty log book from the mine on the desk.

Don Jose picks up the book from the mine and scans the numbers himself, then matches them by month to the log book. His brow furrows before it smooths.

"Who enters these numbers?" I tap the ledger.

"I do," he snaps. "But I don't use these mine logs. I use the reports generated by Don Santiago."

Our eyes meet. *Santiago.* I know both of us are thinking it. Sonofabitch. He must be using the money for whatever hobby science projects he has going. But Don Jose schools his face and says, "Don Santiago knows what's going on. I'm sure these are raw numbers and the one he enters are the final ones. If there's some discrepancy, the council will review it."

I lunge for him, wrapping his shirt up in a fist under his chin. "You're sure? You're sure about a lot, aren't you? You sure about why and how the wealth of this pack has been drained over the past fifty years, leaving the majority of our people in poverty?"

He doesn't struggle, probably because I would win a physical fight. But he doesn't give me the gratification of getting ruffled, maintaining his calm, condescending demeanor. "You're off-balance, Carlos. Get a grip, or we'll have to medicate you, like your mother."

I slam his head down on the desk, cracking his nose. When I lift him, blood pours over his lips and down his chin. I bring my face right up to his. "*Try it,*" I growl. "Try it and I'll kill every last one of you motherfuckers."

Don Jose gives a forced laugh as he gropes for a handkerchief in his pocket. "You are deranged, Carlos."

"Am I, Jose?" I drop the "Don," because he doesn't deserve the respect it implies. "I'm going to keep turning over rocks until I uncover where half the wealth of our mountain has gone. And you'd better pray I don't link its disappearance to the council."

I turn to stalk out and Don Jose pinches his nose with the handkerchief.

My fight for control has begun.

~.~

CARLOS

I HEAD down to the mine to return the logbook. I'm ashamed I haven't spent much time in the mines. I don't know all that goes into it, nor the names and faces of the men who work there. I find Guillermo, the foreman who gave me the logbook working right beside the rest of them.

The mine consists mostly of silver and lead, but originally, when our Spanish ancestors settled here, they mined gold from it, as well.

Guillermo straightens when I come in. He's a huge wolf, face prematurely lined and craggy with hard work. He gives me an up and down sweep of his eyes, taking in my neatly pressed, fine Italian slacks and button down. I look as out of place as a flower in a shit pile here. His eyes land on my collar, and I pull it away from my face to see what he's looking at.

Oh yeah. Some of Don Jose's blood splattered on it. I don't offer any explanation—I don't have to, I'm alpha.

I hold up the log book. "I brought back the records."

Guillermo takes it. I swear I see suspicion under his neutral gaze, but I don't know what it's for. "You find anything... interesting?"

I nod.

I'm not sure how much to share. I don't know who is working for the thief or thieves. I can't say if any wolf here would side with me when I try to bring him or them down. My guess is that the council's behind it, but I need more proof.

"Numbers don't match the council's reports." I opt for the truth and watch the faces around me absorb it.

Some look wary, some angry. Most keep their faces carefully blank, like they're used to covering their thoughts.

Guillermo crosses his arms over his massive chest. "My numbers are good."

"I have no doubt. If anyone here was stealing silver from the pack, you sure as hell wouldn't report it in that log book."

"Stealing from the pack or the council?" one of them mutters. I can't tell who spoke because they all drop their eyes, as if afraid I'll get aggressive.

"The council doesn't own the mountain, the pack does. The wealth that comes out of these mines should be for the benefit of all." I'm campaigning now. If I'm going to make changes around here, I'll need support.

None of them show any response to my words.

"Where's your female?" someone toward the back asks.

The question hits me like a blow to the gut. I could've handled any inquiry, was prepared for any discussion but this one.

Carajo.

The pack wants an alpha with a female. They need to know I'm preserving our alpha line. It's what the council told me, but now I'm seeing how much it matters to them.

Goddammit.

A leader doesn't blame others when he's found lacking. I'm not going to throw the council under the bus, even though I believe their interference ruined my chances with Sedona.

Sedona—*fates.* I've gone all day trying not to think of her, but now she's here, right in the forefront of my mind, the way I last saw her. Hurt, angry, and afraid. Her face pale with fury, blue eyes flashing. *My Sedona.* I nearly double over with the pain that seizes my gut.

I clear my throat. "I'm working on finding a mate. I promise I will take one soon to continue the Montelobo line."

The wolves shift on their feet, and the scent of suspicion grows stronger. They know a bullshit line when they hear one, I guess.

I owe them more credit. Despite the pain in my chest, I try again. "You may have heard I took a mate over the last moon, and it's true. But my mate was brought here against her will, stolen from her pack in America. I refuse to keep her prisoner here. I released her."

Unbelievably, some of the wolves nod, as if they agree with my decision. Maybe all they need is communication from me, so they understand the decisions their alpha is making. Rather than let the guilt at my failing as an alpha drag me under, I plow forward, give them more.

"I know I've been a poor alpha to you. I've been away while conditions here worsened. But I'm back now. I'm ready to dedicate myself to improving Monte Lobo for the good of all, not just those who live in the hacienda." I wave a hand toward the log book. "I'm starting with the finances. Some things don't add up, but I'm going to track where our money is going. Our pack should have greater wealth to make improvements here. Plumbing and electricity for everyone, for starters."

Again, I sense suspicion. Or maybe it's skepticism. How can I fault them? I'm unproven as an alpha.

I try one last time. "My door is open. If you have anything to report, or request, visit me at the hacienda. I want to hear from you."

A few men nod.

I incline my head slightly and turn to walk out of the mine, with the weight of at least twenty pairs of eyes on me.

"*Señor!*" someone calls as I step into the sun. I shield my eyes, blinking until I make out the weathered face. It's Marisol, the old farmer Paco's wife.

"Don Carlos, welcome home." She bobs a curtsey.

"*Señora,*" I greet her. At least someone is glad to see me.

She steps closer. "My husband tells me not me to bother you, but..." She trails off, biting her lip.

"You are one of my pack. You are always welcome to approach me."

The older wolf studies me. I catch a whiff of her emotions—worry, resignation, a tinge of something more than nervousness. Terror?

"You have nothing to fear from me," I emphasize.

"Your father—he was a good wolf," she whispers. "He wanted what's best for the pack. And you—you are like him. We see him in you."

I didn't expect this, so I stay silent.

She drops her gaze, shoulders hunching in submission. "I don't mean any disrespect, alpha."

"Marisol." I touch her shoulder. "I am grateful you spoke. I hope to honor my father's memory." I search for the words. "I also want what's best for the pack. Not a few wolves, but all of them. I promise I will work hard to be the alpha you deserve." I lean close. "Things are going to change around here. For the better." *Whether the council likes it or not.* One day, the pack might rally behind me. Until then, I will work to win their trust.

The hope on Marisol's face tells me that day might soon come.

"Bless you, Don Carlos," she whispers, dropping another curtsey. I let her slip away.

I meant every word I said. Now all I can do is fulfill my promises.

Even if I don't have the motivation of making things perfect for Sedona.

Even if I'm not sure how my heart will go on beating without her.

I will throw myself into my work and make a difference for my pack. And someday, maybe, I can try again with my lovely mate.

13

S *edona*

MY FATHER and I drive two hours up to Flagstaff to visit Rosa, the shifter from Mexico. I fiddle with the radio, but every station gives me a headache. For four days I've lived in a stupor. The pregnancy makes me tired—I sleep fifteen hours a night—but some of the fatigue must be depression.

I see the worried glances my parents exchange when they think I'm not looking. Everyone treats me like I'm made of glass. It's exactly what I didn't want when I first came back from Mexico. Fates, I feel even worse now than I did then.

I was confused, then. Now I'm wrecked. Carlos ruined me for all other males. Ruined me for love. I seriously don't see any light in my future.

No, that's not true. I have this baby to look forward to. At least that gives me purpose.

We pull up to a tiny cabin out in the woods. It's a sweet domicile for a wolf—all of Flagstaff is, a small town surrounded by mountains and woods.

A short, sturdy Latina woman comes out onto the wooden porch, wiping her hands on a dishcloth. She watches me get out of the car with a steady gaze.

My father marches over and shakes her hand. For some reason, my heart's beating faster than normal. She's a little sliver of Carlos—someone from his pack.

I follow my father up the steps and into her little cabin. She waves us into seats at her round kitchen table, which is nestled in a corner under a big picture window. Her back-yard sports a few pine trees and a dog house. The dog, a black lab, is parked right beneath the window, sitting politely, ears cocked and tail wagging.

She pours coffee and brings a carton of half and half to the table, along with a bowl of sugar. I dump two spoonfuls of sugar in my coffee and pour enough milk to turn it blond.

"So," Rosa says, sitting down with us at last. "How can I help you?"

"As I said on the phone, my daughter was taken by the Monte Lobo pack. We have her back, but we want to know everything you can tell us about them."

"They took you for their alpha? As a prize?"

"Yes." I clear my throat. "For Carlos."

"Carlos, yes. I remember him, of course."

She doesn't go on, but my father and I both wait, leaving the space as an invitation.

"I'll start by telling you why I left. You must have seen the disparity between the rich and poor."

I nod.

"I was one of the poor. My father worked in the mines, my mother worked agriculture. It was a good enough life, I didn't know any differently. I mated young, followed in my parents' footsteps.

"I had a hard time keeping a pregnancy. I only carried one pup to full term and even though he was perfect, to me, when he hit puberty, we found out he couldn't shift. Happened to a lot of pups in that generation—too much inbreeding, I know now. We were all related in that pack. Don Santiago, one of the council members, took him from me. Said he could make him better. He drove him down to Mexico City But he never brought him back."

Her eyes fill with tears. "He said he didn't survive the procedure. When my husband raised a fuss, he was crushed in a mining accident."

My father leans forward. "Are you implying it wasn't an accident?"

She shrugs. "Any pack member who made waves disappeared in the mines. It's an easy way to get rid of troublemakers."

A growl sounds in the room. At first I think it must be my dad, then I realize it's coming from me.

"There are alphas who rule their packs with an iron fist, who punish their pack members, even mete out death as a consequence. As wolves, we follow, we obey. It's in our nature. But nothing about that council is natural."

The hairs stand up on my arms. I growl again.

"Sneaky deaths, silent deaths—it keeps the pack afraid, and quiet. The council's spies are everywhere. No one speaks up, for fear they might be next. But after my husband died, I knew I had to leave. My sister, Marisol, helped me escape. She wouldn't leave her husband, but she told me to get out while I still could."

"What about the alpha?" my father asks. "Couldn't you go to him for help?

"They killed him."

My mouth drops open. Carlos hadn't told me that. Did he know?

"If they can't control an alpha, he dies. All they care about his keeping the alpha blood line pure. They don't care about actually having an alpha to rule. Your Carlos, he's in danger now."

"Now?"

She nods, her eyes haunted. "Now that you're pregnant. They'll have no need for him."

~.~

MY LEGS ARE weak when we get back in the car. I knew Carlos' pack was troubled, but I never considered he might be in danger.

But I should have. They had so little respect for him, they caged him in a cell with me. Their own alpha. My mate is in danger. The father of my pup.

My hands shake as I pull out my phone.

"Who are you calling?" My dad's watching me with concern.

"Garrett."

"Why?"

I shake my head impatiently and dial the number.

"Hey sis. Everything okay?"

"Yeah. No, not really. Hey, could you text me Amber's phone number?"

I can practically hear my brother grind his teeth. "You gonna tell me what this is about?"

"I just want to check out some information Dad and I got from a shifter up in Flag. She's from Carlos' pack."

"Okay. But just know that Amber's not entirely comfortable with her gifts yet, and she doesn't like to be put on the spot."

"Isn't that what you did with her to find me?"

"Yeah, smart ass, it is. Never mind. You're both adults, you can work it out between the two of you."

"Thanks."

"Let me know how I can help, okay, sis?"

"Yeah, I will."

"You coming back to your apartment here? We've got you all moved in."

I glance over at my dad, who scowls at the road. Of course he's heard every word. "Maybe. I don't know. I have a lot to figure out."

"I know." His voice is soft with sympathy, which I don't want, so I hit the end button, quickly.

When he texts me the number, I hit dial right away. Amber answers in her professional voice, "Amber Drake speaking."

"Hi Amber, it's Sedona."

"Hi Sedona. What's up?"

"Can I ask you a question? A yes or no one?"

Amber's silent a moment, and I'm sure she's thinking of how to politely tell me to stop using her this way, but she says, "I can try."

"Is Carlos in danger?"

She's quiet for a moment, then I hear her suck in her breath. "Mortal danger," she chokes.

"Fuck," I mutter. "Thank you. Thanks a lot. I appreciate it." I hang up.

My dad frowns. "I knew I should've torn that pack apart the day we picked you up."

"No, Dad," I snap. "Because you would've taken down Carlos, too. And none of this is his fault."

My dad's brows draw together. "We'll go back. Take out just the council. Then you're free to make the right choice about your ma—about Carlos. I don't want your decisions clouded by fear for your safety or your pup's or even the pup's father."

I nod mutely. This is why I love my dad, as much of a controlling ass as he can be. He takes care of things.

Carlos would do this much for our daughter, too. For some reason, I'm suddenly certain our pup is a girl. His vision of the pack has been obscured by lies from the council. If he knew they killed his father, I can't imagine he wouldn't take swift action. He's not a coward, not my Carlos. He's just concerned with doing the right thing for his pack.

And for me. I realize with utter clarity the reason he let me go. It's not for lack of caring. It's because he cares enough. Both times I've left, he let me walk. Because he would never hold me against my will.

Tears leak out of my eyes, but unlike the ones I've cried over the past several days, these aren't full of self-pity. My chest is filled with love. Love for my mate, for Carlos.

And he's in danger now.

Yes, I believe my dad can take care of the council, but I want to be there first. To tell Carlos what I know, and help him sort things out before my dad comes in with the big guns. I can't tell my dad, though, he'd never allow it.

Tonight. As soon as I get back to Phoenix, I'll find a flight out.

14

C *arlos*

"CARLOS, THEY TOOK HIM FROM ME," my mother wails. I'm in her room and she's pacing up and down in front of the window, stopping every now and then to look out.

"No, I'm right here, Mamá." I put my hands on her shoulders and try to catch her gaze.

"Your *father*," she whispers. "They took your father."

"Papi's dead. Remember? An accident in the mine."

She shakes her head rapidly. "No, no accident. They *took* him."

I sigh and look over at Maria Jose, ringing her hands in the corner. "Should we sedate her?"

For a second, I catch a glimpse of judgement in Maria Jose's expression and I'm taken aback. Then I remember what she told me last time.

"You think the drugs make her worse. I haven't had her

checked out yet." I stab my fingers through my hair. "I'm sorry. I'll take her to the city tomorrow. Don Santiago's absence makes it easier to get a second opinion."

Maria Jose's eyes widen and she steps forward. "Yes, yes, Don Carlos. That would be good. Get her away from here. She's not safe—"

She stops speaking and I catch horror on her face before she turns away.

My instincts sharpen, vision tunnels like I'm about to shift. I force myself to remain gentle as I go to her and take her shoulders to turn her around. "What do you mean, she's not safe?"

She shakes her head rapidly. "Nothing, *señor*. Nothing."

I tighten my grip. "Don't lie. *Never* lie to me," I growl. When I see the whites of her eyes grow, I force myself to release her, take a breath. I won't get anywhere going in heavy. "Maria Jose, this is my *mother* we're talking about. I need to know what you meant."

"The drugs—" She wrings her hands again. "What if the drugs *make* her crazy—not the other way around?"

I look at my mother, standing in her white and pink floral nightgown and yellow housecoat, watching us with uncertainty. It's been so long since she's been normal, but I glimpse her old self there now. As if she *wants* to understand what we're saying. She almost does.

"Think about it, when did the craziness start?" Maria Jose whispers.

"After my father died. She was grieving—" I break off when Maria Jose gives a slight shake of her head.

"Think about what she says about your father's death."

They took him from me.

It hits me like a bullet to the head. "They're keeping her quiet."

Maria Jose takes a step back, like she can't believe what she's done.

I stalk to the dresser where her medicines are stacked up and shove them all to the floor. "Get rid of these. No more medicine until she's been checked out. And don't leave her alone for a second. Does anyone but Don Santiago ever inject her?"

Marie Jose shakes her head.

"Good. I don't want anyone going near her. No one but you, understand?"

"Yes, Don Carlos." She bobs her head approvingly.

I look back over at my mother. She appears almost lucid, like she understands what we're saying. She points with a shaking hand to the floor by her bed.

"What is it, Mamá?"

Fates, the Parkinson's-like tremors in her hands break my heart. A side-effect of the drugs.

My mother rushes over and drops to her knees on the floor.

Carajo. More craziness.

"Mamá, get off the floor. It's oka—" I stop when I see she's prying one of the floorboards up.

"What's in there, Mamá?" I look a question at Maria Jose, who shakes her head.

Gently lifting my mother to sit on the bed, I pull up the board and look underneath. There are hundreds of pills in a rainbow of colors and varying sizes. But underneath is a journal. I remember it from when I was a kid. My mom used to write poetry in it and read it to me. Is this a moment of nostalgia, or is she showing me something significant?

I look over my shoulder at her, but her expression is simple and vacant.

I pull out the journal, shaking off the pills and tuck it in my pocket. I don't know if she's trying to tell me something or if this is more of her crazy, but I'm taking it with me for safekeeping.

I bend and kiss my mom on the top of the head and nod at Maria Jose. "Pack a bag for both of you. We'll leave in the morning."

When I see Maria Jose hesitate, I guess her fear. "We'll bring Juanito, too. I will keep you both safe, I promise."

She relaxes and dips into a curtsy. "Thank you, Señor."

~.~

Sedona

BY SOME MIRACLE, I find a flight to Mexico City going out tonight and call an Uber to meet me at a block from my parents' house. The last thing I want to do is get some pack member in trouble for driving me to the airport and I know my dad would never let me leave. I slip out of the house with nothing more than a backpack, because—yeah—a suitcase might signal to my family that I'm going somewhere.

I know they'll be on my tail, and that's fine. I just want to get there first.

I board the plane, strong with determination. I'm not letting anyone take my pup's father from her. Or from me. It's funny how things become crystal clear when you stand to lose it all.

I won't lose Carlos. He's mine. My mate. The father of

my pup. He has an enormous heart—cares deeply for his mother, the little servant boy who set me free, his pack.

For me.

It's so obvious now to me how much he both cares for and respects me. He worshipped my body, dominated me, but still gave me my congress. I'm not willing to live without him.

I don't know how we'll make it work, but we'll figure something out. If the council is eliminated from the picture, my trauma and resentments from my captivity could be put to rest. I'd be willing to help him make the changes he envisions for his pack. If we worked together, I have no doubt we could do great things there.

Look what my brother did in Tucson with just a little startup capital and a ragtag pack of young males. Now he has a thriving real estate business, a nightclub, and a strong, loyal pack, willing to do anything for him. And a mate. Having Amber will change things even more—I can't wait to see how. Maybe they'll provide a cousin for our pup.

But I'm getting way ahead of myself. I have to save Carlos first.

The rest, we'll figure out.

~.~

CARLOS

I WAKE up with my head on my desk, drool running down my chin. I must've fallen asleep reviewing the books. I spent the night pouring through more financial journals, following the trails of money. Since Don Santiago was the only tech-savvy member of *el consejo*, he's been the one to handle the on-line accounts. He appears to be the one stealing from the pack. Whether it's with the complicity of *el consejo* or not, I can't be sure.

I swore for a moment, I saw surprise in Don Jose's eyes when I told him what I'd found, but he quickly covered it up. That was what pissed me off. *El consejo* always operates alone, without bringing me in on discussions or decisions. I know that's not how it should be.

My father was a member of the council. I remember him being locked in the conference room for long hours, coming out looking beaten down and haggard, angry and stressed by whatever discussion they'd had.

I haven't even been invited in on such meetings. I'm ready to disband the whole fucking council. If I thought I had support from the pack, I'd do it today. This minute. Before I drive my mom down to *el D.F.*

Which reminds me—I never looked at her journal. I pull it out of my pocket and skim through the pages. It's what I remembered—poetry, quotes. Snippets of beauty my mother liked to share with me.

I thumb toward the back of the journal. Does she still write in this thing? I wouldn't think she'd even be capable with her shaky hands and addled brain. No. The last entries are dated fifteen years ago.

Which would be around the time of my father's death. I slow down and read. Her handwriting is messier, as if writing in a hurry, or under duress. The ink on the last pages is smeared with tears.

· · ·

My mate, my Carlos disappeared today. How will I go on without him? How can this be? I know who killed him. It's as plain to me as day.

The argument with the council last night had gone on late. When he came back, he told me they seized control over all the monetary assets, told him he is no longer allowed to make financial decisions for the pack. He was furious. He paced in the bedroom all night and left early this morning, but he never returned.

Don Jose says there was an accident in the mine, but I know it's a lie. They killed him, just like they kill everyone who goes up against them. Everyone knows there's a pile of bodies in that mine. Every young shifter who might be a physical threat. Every wolf who dissents on any point. Any male or female who doesn't toe the line.

Everyone lives in fear here. I only have one choice—to get Carlitos out of here before he becomes their next victim. If only I knew who I could trust.

Ice sluices through my veins as I read.

The council killed my father. I always thought it was an accident in the mine. Like so many others. But my mother suspected none of them were accidents.

Are these simply the ravings of a madwoman? They don't seem it. Paranoid, perhaps. But fully coherent. Logical. They must have offered the first drugs to her as something to calm her down, ease her grieving. Then they kept her silent all these years.

But why not just kill her? Wouldn't that be easier than keeping her around? Perhaps they feared it would arouse too much suspicion.

I jump to my feet and go to my mother's room first, fear for her safety suddenly spiking through me.

I find Maria Jose has her dressed, bag packed and ready.

"She's eaten breakfast, we're ready any time."

"They started drugging her—when? Immediately after my father's dead?"

Recognition sparks in Maria Jose's eyes. She knows what I know. She nods.

"And my mother suspected them of killing my father. Did you know that?"

Again, she nods.

"So they've silenced her with drugs that made her mad?"

"I fear it's so, Don Carlos."

"Wait here. Lock the door. Don't allow anyone in but me. Understand?"

She bobs her head. "*Sí, señor.*"

I pound down the white marble steps and find Don Jose eating breakfast with Don Mateo on the upper terrace.

His broken nose has already healed, which makes me want to break it again. I grab Mateo this time. "What happened to my father? The truth."

"A mine shaft collapsed. You know that." Mateo keeps his eyes lowered, doesn't pull the condescending bullshit Jose always tries.

My wolf is close to the surface, ready to tear out and kill all threats. I shake him. "Bullshit. You had him killed. How did you arrange it?"

Servants gather in the doorway to watch. Out of the corner of my eye, I see Juanito in the shadows. My need to protect him makes me rougher with Mateo.

"My mother knew and you started drugging her. The drugs make her crazy, not the other way around."

"Calm yourself, Carlos," Jose placates. "Your mother isn't

well, and neither are you." His cell phone buzzes and he pulls it out and looks at the screen. "We have a security issue at the gate."

That's probably a lie, but I pull back, because I realize I'm playing right into Don Jose's game of making me the crazy one. I have no proof but a raving woman's diary. What I do have proof of, is financial misdeeds.

I release Mateo and straighten my jacket. Servants have gathered to watch the proceedings, along with a few pack members. I see Marisol out of the corner of my eye and she appears to be sending her husband Paco out, possibly to gather others.

I have an audience now, it's time to make a declaration. "I'm taking over the finances of this pack. Someone has siphoned off half the profits of the mine going back at least ten years and I'm going to find out who. Anyone—*everyone* —who played a role in the theft *or covering it up* will be punished. Severely."

That causes a stir amongst the servants. Mateo's gone pale. Now for the *coup de grâce*.

"I'm also disbanding the council." My raised voice carries across the expanse of the terrace, out into the land beyond.

The audible gasps and murmurs circulate. Wolves have appeared all around, listening out windows, drawing near from the gardens and fields. I see Paco hustling back, followed by Guillermo and his men from the mine. They are the strongest wolves. If there is a fight, they will be the ones to win it. I wish I knew which way they'd swing.

"This happened under your watch. Our pack grows poorer, sicker. Weaker. You cannot be trusted to protect the best interest of the wolves here. As alpha, that's my job, and it's one I accept. Your assistance in leading the pack is no longer wanted, nor accepted."

The sound of a vehicle climbing the road to the citadel rumbles.

Jose gives a loud, fake laugh. "Boy, you think this pack would ever give control over to you—an untried, unpracticed youth—to lead, you're as deranged as your mother. You may have alpha blood, but you don't have what it takes to make the hard decisions."

The other two council members arrive, walking swiftly, straightening their ties and jackets. "What is all this?" Don Julio asks.

"The council has been disbanded. Anyone who questions my authority will be banished. Is that clear enough?" I shout, making sure everyone can hear. "Who's first?" I make a beckoning motion with my hand and sweep my gaze to encompass every wolf around. I'm ready to fight, in human or wolf form.

"The boy's gone mad!" Don Jose proclaims loudly. "He's dangerous. Grab him and put him in the dungeons."

It's on.

Three of council's lackey servants strip to shift. The four members of the council advance on me. Alone, I could take any of them. Probably even all seven. But will the others stay back to watch? Or will they join in?

Out of the corner of my eye, I see Guillermo taking off his boots, preparing to fight. I guess I'll find out which side he's picked. Growling, I tear off my shirt and yank down my pants, shifting the minute my clothes are off.

Growls erupt all around. I leap, not waiting for the elders to strip and shift. Not waiting for the pack to choose sides. The warning bell tolls, calling all the pack in to join the melee.

I take down one of the council's lackeys, and knock his flying body into another. I tear deep into his shoulder. We roll on the ground but he doesn't give the submissive whine to signal defeat. To the death, then. I release my jaws, adjust and sink into his throat. Two other wolves attack me from both sides, but Guillermo's wolf knocks one of them down, snapping his neck with a crunch of bone. I tear the flesh of the third wolf.

In a blur of movement, every pack member prepares to shift. Wasting no time, I flip up to my feet and lunge for the council elders, who seem to think they're exempt from the fight. I launch into the air for Don Mateo.

Shots ring out and pummel my chest. Too late, I see the gun in Mateo's hand. My body twists in the air. I lose my breath and my bearings and land on my side. Snarls and yips—the sounds of a full wolf fight—fill the air.

Before my vision clears, I spring up again, snarling, fully expecting attack from the wolves closing in from all directions. A blur of white fur flashes in front of me. I lunge on instinct, then whine and twist away so fast I skid out on the blood pooling on the marble.

Sedona.

Somehow, my white wolf is here, fangs bared, feet planted in front of me.

No, it can't be. This is some hallucination. Did I die from the gunshot wounds?

I scramble back to my feet, vision swimming. A tight circle of fur and legs closes around us only—can it be?—the wolves are facing out, away from us. They're protecting their alpha and his mate.

His *pregnant* mate.

I snarl with a furious need to protect her when I realize the change in Sedona's scent. I spin in a circle, checking all around for danger, but we're completely protected. She growls at my side, fucking magnificent. Bigger, healthier than any wolf here.

The ferocious sounds of wolves fighting to the death reaches my ears but I can't see over the wall of wolves guarding us. It goes against my nature to let others fight for me. I nip at the flanks of my guards to get through and they reluctantly fall back, dropping to their bellies as I pass to show deference.

The terrace teams with wolves and those in human form, who cannot shift. Every pack member must be here, the mines and fields empty. Dead bodies strew the terrace. One, two, three... nine. All the councilmembers, minus Don Santiago, who hasn't returned from Europe. Some of their closest lackeys and guards. Others are being chased away by small packs, the whine and yip of the hunt carrying away from us now.

My body is weak, but I'm careful not to show it. I sit on my haunches and howl. Voices lift all around me, mating with mine, answering my call. Gratitude pours from my being as the sense of oneness, of pack, of family joins us all.

I wheel around and limp back to Sedona, who's still trying to nip her way out of the protective ring of wolves. When they see me coming, they once more go down on their bellies and she rushes out, meets me halfway. We whine and lick and circle each other and every wolf there drops down, honoring us.

Their alphas.

If I can convince Sedona to stay.

15

S *edona*

JUANITO TAKES away the bloody towels and spreads a blanket over Carlos. I curl up on the bed with him because it's the only way I can get him to stay lying down. He refuses to be parted from me, won't take his eyes off me for a second.

I twitch the blanket higher over his mostly naked form. He did put on boxer briefs in deference to his mother, who insisted on sponging the blood from him. She appeared lucid to me, although she did babble a lot about a wolf fight that I think must've been in the past.

Carlos reaches for me, and I nestle closer so he doesn't have to move. "Just lie still and let your body take care of the bullet wounds," I chide.

Shifters have incredible healing capabilities, but in such a serious case like Carlos', with major blood loss, it takes a few days of rest. Or at the very least, a night.

We're nose to nose and he strokes my hair back from my face, leaning his forehead against mine. "*Mi corazon*, I feared I'd never be this close to you again."

"What does *corazon* mean?"

"My heart. You are my heart. What made you come here?" He strokes a hand over my hip. "Did you come to tell me about our pup?"

I shake my head, experiencing a pang of guilt at keeping that from him the whole time we were in Europe. "Carlos —" I stop, unsure how to tell him what I learned.

He stiffens, like he thinks I'm breaking up with him —again.

"I met a shifter from your pack. She told me the council killed your father." I blurt it out quickly, so he won't have to suffer any suspense.

He nods gravely.

"You knew?"

"No, I discovered last night that my mother believed so. I now think the council drugged her to keep her quiet. I planned to take her to the city today to see a human psychiatrist. I don't know how much permanent damage has been done, but I'm hoping there's a chance her mental faculties can be restored."

"Were all the councilmembers killed today?"

"All but one—Don Santiago, who we saw in Barcelona. He's still away, but I'll deal with him when he returns. He's the one who's been stealing from the pack."

I rub the place my arm had been pricked again. "I think he drew blood from me there."

"*What?*" Carlos surges upright and I have to tug him back down to the mattress.

"When you were talking to him, these humans jostled

up against me and something poked my arm. I think he was testing to see if I'm pregnant."

Carlos' grim face pales. "Santiago... playing doctor with my mother. With you. Interested in gene mapping. Healthy young wolves disappearing from this pack—like Juanito's brother and father. Huge amounts of money disappearing... Could he be the so-called *Harvester*?"

I shiver involuntarily. "There were lots of cages in the warehouse where I was held. Many wolves had been prisoner there. And they took my brother and his pack mates prisoner rather than killing them. You think he's... experimenting on shifters?"

"I do." Carlos surges off the bed and onto his feet.

Fates, he's pushing himself too hard. "Carlos, wait. He's not here now—it can wait. Or do what you need to do in bed. With me." I add the last part on and waggle my eyebrows and his expression softens into a smile. He sinks back down onto the bed. "Well if you put it that way..." His palm lands right on my ass and he squeezes a handful.

But his smile falls away again and he pins me with his gaze. "Tell me, Sedona. Can you ever forgive me? Forgive my pack?"

"Yes. I know you had nothing to do with it. And the council is now gone. I should tell you—my father and brother and their packs will be here soon." I texted my dad when I landed last night. He let me know they were right behind me, on a flight this morning. I pull out my phone to text again and let him know I'm safe. "After we talked to the shifter from your pack, he believed me to be in danger from the council, so he's coming to help you clean house. I'll let him know it's already done."

"Then he will be here for our mating ceremony." Carlos'

tone is light, but he watches me closely and I don't think he's breathing.

I throw a leg up over his. "I believe we're already mated."

His smile flashes, sexy and winsome. "Does that mean yes? You'll have me as your mate?"

My nod wobbles a bit. "We'll figure it out."

"Of course." Carlos sobers. "I would never keep you here if you cannot find joy. But I promise I will work very hard to keep you happy, *mi amor*. And if you wish to split your time with the States, I understand that, too. You'll be like Persephone, taking a break from hell."

"No," I answer immediately. "My place is with you. I mean, yes, I want to visit home, but there's nothing there for me. Not without you. And this place isn't hell. It's beautiful. A paradise, Carlos."

He blinks rapidly. "Thank you," he chokes and takes my face in both hands, stamping his lips over mine, stealing my breath. "I think it can be a paradise. It's a fixer upper, but if I'm working for you, there's nothing I can't do. Fates, I can't believe it. I feared I wouldn't manage to keep you."

"I'm here," I whisper.

He kisses me again. "I see you, *preciosa. Gracias.*"

I gaze into his warm chocolate brown eyes, feel the love pouring from him. "When I thought you were in danger, all the walls I'd erected, all the fears and insecurities about whether you really loved me, or if it was just your biology insisting you follow because you'd marked me fell away. I knew I wouldn't want to know a future without you in it, that I'd be willing to die to protect you. So I'm here."

"*Muñeca*, yes, there's biology—fates, *so much*—but my love for you goes way beyond the physical. You are everything that's beautiful in the world. And I know I don't know everything about you yet—I don't know your favorite song, or movie, or television show, I haven't met your family, yet, I don't know your childhood stories. But I do know that I crave every part of you, even the parts you keep hidden." His hand curves around my nape and pulls my face to his. He kisses me with a soft, exploratory movement of his lips over mine.

Heat surges through my body, but I do my best to ignore it. Carlos needs to heal. Jumping his bones definitely won't help. There will be time for that tomorrow.

He must pick up my vibe, because his eyes smolder when he pulls away. "Don't think you won't be punished for putting yourself in danger out there, *ángel*. It's not your job to protect me. I would much rather die than ever see you hurt."

And just like that, my pussy is dripping. It's all I can do not to close the distance between our hips and grind against the bulge in his boxer briefs. I can't stop my lids from dropping to half-mast. My tongue runs over my lips. "How will you punish me, Carlos?"

His cock punches out to a full erection, tenting his shorts and he yanks my body up against his hard muscles. "You're lucky you're clothed or I'd already be inside you," he growls.

I push against his chest, but he doesn't give me any freedom—not that I wanted it. "Easy, big wolf. You still have five holes in your gut."

He squeezes my ass and wedges a finger between the cleft, working deeper until he presses against my back hole through my pants. "Tomorrow, *muñeca*. Tomorrow I'm going to fuck this ass until you scream. *That's* your punishment."

A tiny whimper escapes my lips as my entire body lights on fire, flames sizzling right down to my toes. I bite his bulging pectoral muscle. "Promise?"

16

Carlos

I WAKE with Sedona in my arms. I bury my nose in her thick hair and breathe in her scent. Somehow, I managed to actually sleep with her beside me and I didn't even have to tie her to the bedpost and fuck her senseless.

It must have been the bullet wounds and my body's need to heal.

Although my dick is rock hard, I don't move, content to simply watch my mate sleep. I've already marked her, but today she'll become mine in front of my pack and hers. Her mother and Garrett's mate are even flying out this morning to witness it.

Yesterday's cluster-fuck ended up better than I could've wished for. Sedona's father and brother spent a good ninety minutes giving me the third degree, but I think they finally conceded that I love Sedona and would give my life to protect her and make her happy.

We spent last night initiating a worldwide search for Santiago, who I believe must be "the Harvester." According to a hacker friend of Garrett, Santiago has gone dark. The hacker friend found every bank account he's associated with and issued a fake FBI freeze on the funds. She also removed him from every pack financial account, so I hope with his financial support cut off, his activities will be quickly curtailed. Sedona's father and brother vow to continue the hunt for him.

Sedona's lids blink open and those azure eyes train on my face. Her soft lips part and she leans forward. I think she's going to kiss my neck, but she bites it. Hard.

Laughter rockets from my throat as I flip her onto her back and pin her hands above her head. "Someone's ready for her punishment."

She blushes and squirms, but the flare of her pupils and scent of her arousal tells me I'm right.

Fates, how did I get so lucky?

I nudge her legs apart with my knee, and bite her shoulder.

"Are you sure you're up for it?" She peers innocently up from under her lashes.

I growl and roll her to her side, applying my hand to her backside several times. Nothing pisses an alpha off more than the assumption he's not up for something.

She giggles and wiggles her ass. She's wearing a pair of panties and one of my t-shirts, which my wolf finds tremendously satisfying. "Get up. Use the bathroom, if you need to. Take off your clothes. I'll deal with your misbehavior when you return."

She shoots out of bed, excitement evident in her race to

the bathroom and her quick shower. She emerges damp and naked.

Growls start up in my throat the moment I see her naked body, which she throws at me from across the room, tackling me down to the mattress when I catch her. I flip her to her tummy and pin both hands behind her back. "Leave these here. Don't even think about moving them, or I'll double the punishment."

"Yes, sir."

A blast of lust pounds through me at her submissive response. She's so hot.

I pull her hips up until she's on her knees, her face pressed into the mattress. "Get those legs wide." My voice has never sounded so low.

She spreads her knees apart and I grip the tops of her thighs and pull them open, parting her wide. I lick into her, parting her outer lips with my tongue, tracing the inner ones.

Her pussy drips honey and I lap it up, tonguing her clit. Her thighs quake. I drag my tongue up to her anus, rimming her as I slap between her legs.

She cries out, a wanton, needy sound and I continue, spanking her wet pussy as I lick her anus. "No, no more. Oh fates, yes. Please, Carlos."

I spank harder, faster, until she comes, arms flying off her back, knees snapping closed.

I change my attack, spanking her sweet ass, all the way through her orgasm, following when she flops flat on the bed, body soft and pliant from her release.

I turn her ass red, and the pain must set in, because she whimpers, twisting her head around. "I'm sorry! I'm sorry, Carlos."

I fall on her immediately, squeezing and rubbing her

chastened cheeks as I kick her legs apart. I kiss a trail up her back, admiring the slender lines, the lean feminine muscle of my alpha she-wolf.

We could be mated for eighty years and she'd still steal my breath with her beauty. I caress her nape, move her hair to one side to bite her ear. "Don't move," I murmur.

I scramble to grab some lube, still packed in the bag from Europe. When I return, I pull her cheeks apart and squeeze a dollop on her anus. Using a medium-sized buttplug, I stretch her opening. She whimpers and moans as I twist and pump it inside of her.

"What comes now, Sedona?"

Her bottom squeezes around the plug. "I-I don't know."

"Yes you do." I give each cheek a smack. "What am I going to do to you now, *ángel*?"

"F-fuck my ass?"

I grip each of her cheeks roughly, squeezing and separating them. "That's right, *mi amor*." I pull out the medium plug and apply more lube. I coat my throbbing cock, too. This might be punishment but there will be no pain, only pleasure.

"You're going to take it, you know why?"

"No."

"Yes, you do. Because you were a bad girl. You put yourself in danger. That's not allowed, beautiful."

"S-sorry." She's panting, lifting her ass for me, excited.

I straddle her ass and pull her cheeks wide, bump the head of my cock against her back pucker. "Take me."

Somehow, she knows to relax, and the tip of my cock enters. I go slowly, giving her time to get used to it.

She sucks in her breath and bites the bedspread, gathers it up in fists as I inch in.

"Good girl."

"Yes!" she gasps.

I'm not sure what she's saying *yes* to, but I take it as a sign that she's okay and continue, sinking into her.

She's tight, her heat wrapping my dick up like a fist. I won't last long. There's something so taboo, so fucking hot about punishing her this way. I want to pound into her and find my release, but I force myself to keep my movements slow and even.

I shove one hand under her hips and cup her mons. Her swollen, sopping pussy welcomes my fingers. I finger-fuck her with three, shoving my digits deep as my cock withdraws, alternating.

"Please, Carlos, please. Oh fates. Oh yes..." Her cries grow to a high-pitched squeal that never stops.

My breath grows jerky and I plow harder, doing my best to keep the thrusts straight and measured. My eyes roll back in my head, stars explode in my vision. I bury myself deep in her ass and come.

The minute I do, she comes, too, her internal muscles quaking around my fingers. "Carlos, Carlos, Carlos..."

"Keep saying my name, *mi amor*. I'm the only one who's going to make you come."

"Yes!" Another spasm of her pussy.

I bump her ass with a few short thrusts and drop my body over hers, kissing her neck. When our breaths slow, I ease out and roll to my side, wrapping her in my arms, her back to my front. "I love you, beautiful. Love you so much."

She covers my hands with her smaller ones. "I love you, too, Carlos. How do you say it in Spanish?"

"*Te quiero. Te adoro. Te amo.*"

She gives a husky laugh that has my cock hardening again. "All of that. And more."

~.~

SEDONA

I STAND by the entry to the terrace, my hand hooked around my dad's elbow. The terrace has been transformed. The marble gleams, scrubbed clean of the blood from yesterday's fight. Strings of lights twinkle from every banister, every tree. Round tables covered in white linen bedeck the space, and every seat is filled by the members of Carlos' pack, and mine.

The scent of traditional foods fills the air and a long banquet table stands ready with heaps of savory meat, vegetables, fruits, and sweets. I can't wait to try the chicken mole, which Carlos promises is the best in Mexico.

My body's already recovered from Carlos' delicious punishment this morning, but I feel fully claimed by him.

After we made love, he took me, Garrett, and my dad on a tour of the mountain, showing us its incredible beauty and riches and introducing us to his pack members.

My mother and Amber arrived at noon and spent this afternoon helping me prepare. Amber wove a string of seed pearls in with my hair, braiding a crown around the top of my head. The rest she curled into ringlets that hang down my back.

I miraculously fit into my mother's wedding dress, a spaghetti strap white and silver gown with a V that plunges almost to my ass in the back and a more modest matching one pointing to my cleavage in front. Amber lent me a pair of silver strappy sandals. I feel like a princess about to become queen of a new kingdom.

The mariachi band finishes a beautiful ballad and everyone looks expectantly at Carlos, who has stepped to a raised dais in the center by the edge. He looks unbelievably handsome tonight in a tuxedo. He says something grand about me in Spanish. I don't know the words he speaks, but the meaning isn't lost because he stares at me with a reverence that sets my body vibrating.

His.

Every cell in my body knows it. I belong with him. To him.

He turns to the tables of Americans and says, "To say I am honored to take Sedona as my mate would be an understatement. She is my life, my light. The angel who helped me see the way to clear the oppression and corruption that's plagued my pack. I will spend every day of our lives making up for the wrongs done to her here." He makes a point of looking at my father, then my brother as he delivers this.

My father nods, as if he's been waiting for this pronouncement, and he leads me in. We're not having a real wedding ceremony the way some American wolves do. This is just a celebration of the mating that's already taken place. Even so, Juanito, shined up in a suit, holds out a small jewelry box to Carlos and my mate takes out a ring which he slips on the tip of his index finger.

He only has eyes for me as I come toward him. My father stops in front of the raised platform and kisses my cheek. Carlos reaches for my face with both hands, and pulls my mouth up to his, slanting his lips over mine.

I moan softly into his mouth and he smiles against my lips. "I love you, my white wolf." He picks up my hand and slides a slender gold band with three oval emeralds on my finger. "I'll get you a real ring soon, but I wanted to give you something tonight. This was my grandmother's."

It's loose, so I take it off and slide it on my middle finger, instead, where it fits.

He holds both my hands and gazes into my eyes. "Marry me."

I laugh. "Again, I think the deed is already done. I'm wearing the ring." I hold up my hand and wiggle my fingers.

He slides his nose over mine. "I want it all ways—legal marriage, family ceremony, moon-marked."

I press my lips to his. "You have me. I'm in. I'm all in."

Carlos grins and holds up our intertwined hands in a clear gesture of victory, turning to face the tables again. "I have found and claimed my mate. Please, let the feast begin!"

The mariachi strikes up and I lean into Carlos, soak up his presence, so solid and warm. So right.

"I love you, Carlos." He already knows, but it feels important to say it now, in this moment.

He tips my face up and stares down at me without moving.

"What are you doing?"

"Memorizing this moment. I never want to forget how wonderful it feels to know you're mine."

I rise to my toes and stamp my lips over his. "I claim you back, black wolf. You're as much mine as I am yours."

A boyish grin spreads across his face. "Promise?"

THE END

WANT MORE? ALPHA'S CHALLENGE

Please enjoy this short excerpt from the next stand-alone book in the *Bad Boy Alphas* Series, *Alpha's Challenge*

Foxfire

A small pop was my only warning before my soup exploded.

"Dammit." I rip open the microwave door. Only half my tomato soup is left, and the inside of my microwave looks like a murder scene.

Good thing I already ordered a pizza.

With a sigh, I shut the door on the gruesome red spatter. My stomach's gurgling like I haven't eaten in a day. Maybe I haven't. I barely know what day it is. Day Eight of the Break-up From Hell, and the only thing keeping me connected to the outside world is my best friend.

Speaking of best friends... I hit my one and only speed dial number. It goes straight to voicemail, catching me by surprise. Amber should be home, lying low after I rescued her from her own Date from Hell.

I give up the call and shoot off a text, *Just ordered a pizza —come share half?*

It's probably too soon to mention her dating disaster. She'd only known the guy a few days, but he was her neighbor. *Awkward.* And yeah, he was hot, but since when does that give a guy an excuse to abandon a woman on the side of a mountain in the middle of a first date?

My ex is a jackhole, and even he wouldn't do that.

Bring a picture of Garrett. I've got one of Benny, and a bunch of darts... I start to text, and delete it. Instead, I type, *I'm giving up on men forever. Let's get fat and adopt lots of cats.*

There. That'll make her laugh.

I pace around the house, noting piles of mail and take out detritus that appeared over the past few days. Since the break-up, I've been practically a shut in. Benny still hasn't come by, even to pick up his stuff.

Not that I want him to. Rat bastard.

Amber still hasn't texted me back. Weird. It's six p.m. on a Saturday night, but my best friend is usually home, alone. Like me.

Geez, we're pathetic. Maybe we really should adopt some cats.

I text Amber again. *Don't adopt any cats without me.*

My mom was right. Men suck. I'd be happy if I never saw another man for the rest of my life. Except the pizza delivery guy. I'll make an exception for him.

When the doorbell rings, I dash out to the living room and open it, perhaps a wee bit too eager.

"What do I owe—" my voice dies. I look up. And up. And up some more.

Damn, this pizza delivery boy is tall. And stacked. Like "The Rock" or something. Six foot and then some, with shoulders almost too big for the door. Military buzz cut. Mirrored shades on his face... at dusk.

Hey big boy, my foxy bits purr. No! Bad Foxfire!

"Foxfire Hines?" He looks a bit disbelieving, like he can't quite believe that's my name. I get that a lot.

"My mother was a hippie," I say.

"What?" His eyebrows shoot up over the shades.

"My name. It's because... my mom. She thought it was pretty."

"Your mom."

"Yes."

"So your name is really Foxfire." He sounds almost resigned, like he can't believe the turn his life has taken, to deliver him to my door. I understand. I've never pledged my undying lust to a pizza guy. Both of us are having a night of firsts.

"Were you waiting for me?" he asks.

"Uh yeah." Then it hits me, though the cloud of longing. What my brain was screaming over my libido. "Wait... where's the pizza?"

~.~

Tank

Foxfire. Fucking ridiculous. The chick looks as crazy as her name. On paper, she's okay. Graphic designer, good client list, pays her bills on time. Lives in a respectable adobe brick house near the University. So far, so good. In person, she's a walking, talking freak show. Hair dyed in like a rainbow, something out of a cartoon. She's also tiny, a petite pixie in short shorts and strappy tank. I could pick her up and hold her in my hand.

Oh and she's stunning. Even with the clown hair.

This job's either gonna be easy, or huge pain in my ass.

"Where's the pizza?" she asks, peering around me. Before she can protest, I push inside, noting the explosion of papers on every surface, bean bag chairs on the floor, a few dream catchers in the windows and a lava lamp in the corner. The cartoon pixie lives in La La land.

"What are you doing?" She blinks at me, her starry eyes wide. Totally unafraid. A man twice her size just pushed into her house, and she's asking about pizza. Most woman would be freaked.

Not this one.

Like I said, La La land.

"I need to talk to you," I say.

"Okay," she says, and adds in a hopeful tone, "Did you leave the pizza in the car?"

"No pizza. This is about Amber."

"Amber?" Her head snaps back and she sucks in a breath.

"Miss Hines, you better sit down," I say. To my surprise, she drops onto the only decent seat in the place, a battered couch. Responded to authority right away. If she was pack, I'd say she was a feisty, but submissive wolf.

Maybe this is going to easy.

"Is something wrong? Is Amber in trouble?"

"Not yet. Not if you cooperate."

"What?" she whispers, the blood draining from her face. The scent of her fear fills the room, and my wolf raises his head. Because he fucking *hates* it.

It's my turn to suck in a breath. My wolf never pays any attention to humans. Not even pretty females with freaky hair.

"I'm not here to hurt you." Now why did I promise that?

I'm supposed to be intimidating her. My job was to get in, see what this female knew, get her under control. Keep my pack safe. Easy. But now my wolf is all in a tizzy that we might be scaring her. Which is ridiculous. Since when did he care about a human's feelings more than the safety of the pack?

"I'd like this to be quick and painless, but it's up to you. Amber talked to you this afternoon. I need to know what she said."

She stares at me.

"This will go easier if you do as I say," I add.

Immediately her back stiffens. "Did you just threaten me?"

"Miss—"

"Did you hurt Amber? Where is she?" She's on her feet now, voice rising to a shout. This five-foot nothing pixie acts like she's going to challenge me. And my wolf... he thinks she's even cuter when she's mad.

"You better not have touched her, buddy," Foxfire hisses. "I told that moron Garrett, and I'm telling you. When it comes to Amber, back off."

She is challenging me. She also called my alpha a moron. She either is crazy, or suicidal.

"Miss Hines—"

"I meant it." She pokes me in the stomach, and my dominant side surges. I catch her wrist and pull her forward, turning her at the last minute so she ends up tucked against me, back to my front, my body bent over hers and nose buried in her rainbow-colored hair. I catch the scent of her: strawberry shampoo, printer's ink, a bit of hippie incense, and a wild smell that hovers out of reach, familiar, but not something I can place.

She struggles but she's trapped, a slender armful curved

in all the right places. My dick takes this unfortunate moment perk up.

"Let me tell you how this is going to go, sweetheart," I whisper in her ear. "I'm going to ask the questions. You're going to give me answers. And if you're very, very good, you and your friend will be fine. Understand?"

"Let me go." She rears up, stomping her feet on mine. Since mine are encased in biker boots, and hers are bare, it probably hurts her more than it hurts me. I lift her off her feet, and almost take a heel to my dick. I shift her to the side at the last moment, and her foot bounces off my thigh.

"Help, murder! Rape!" Foxfire shrieks. I clamp my hand over her mouth and she bites me. My wolf decides he's in love.

In the next few seconds, we're down on the floor, my hand still over her mouth, my body weight pinning her. An interesting position for doing all sorts of things, my wolf points out. My dick agrees.

I flip her so she's facing me. Her chest rises and falls rapidly, her scent's filled with fear, but her eyes spit fire.

"That's enough." I force enough dominance in my tone to cow a whole pack of wolves. "Are you going to cooperate, or do I have to tie you up?"

She makes a noise against my palm that sounds a lot like *fuck you.* I'm about to tell her I'd love to oblige, when the doorbell rings. The goddam pizza is here.

Maybe this isn't going to be so easy.

~.~

Alpha's Challenge
  How to Date a Werewolf:
  #1 Never call him 'Good Doggie.'

I've got a problem. A big, hairy problem. An enforcer from the Werewolves Motorcycle Club broke into my house. He thinks I know the Werewolves' secret, and the pack sent him to guard me.

#2 During a full moon, be ready to get freaky

By the time he decides I'm no threat, it's too late. His wolf has claimed me for his mate.

Too bad we can't stand each other...

 # 3 Bad girls get eaten in the bedroom

...until instincts take over. Things get wild. Naked under the full moon, this wolfman has me howling for more.

 # 4 Break ups are hairy

Not even a visit from the mob, my abusive ex, my crazy mother and a road trip across the state in a hippie VW bus can shake him.

#5 Beware the mating bite

Because there's no running from a wolf when he decides you're his mate.

Click to read Alpha's Challenge now!

READ ALL THE BAD BOY ALPHA BOOKS

Bad Boy Alphas Series
Alpha's Temptation
Alpha's Danger
Alpha's Prize
Alpha's Challenge
Alpha's Obsession
Alpha's Desire
Alpha's War
Alpha's Mission
Alpha's Bane
Alpha's Secret
Alpha's Prey
Alpha's Blood
Alpha's Sun

Shifter Ops
Alpha's Moon
Alpha's Vow
Alpha's Revenge

Midnight Doms
Alpha's Blood
His Captive Mortal
Additional books by other authors

WANT FREE BOOKS?

Go to reneeroseromance.com to sign up for Renee Rose's newsletter and receive a free copy of *Theirs to Protect, Owned by the Marine, Theirs to Punish, The Alpha's Punishment, Disobedience at the Dressmaker's* and *Her Billionaire Boss*. In addition to the free stories, you will also get special pricing, exclusive previews and news of new releases.

Go to www.leesavino.com to sign up for Lee Savino's awesomesauce mailing list and get a FREE Berserker book —too hot to publish anywhere else!

ACKNOWLEDGMENTS

Thank you to Aubrey Cara, Katherine Deane, Miranda, and Margarita for their beta reads!

Read all the books in the *Bad Boy Alphas* Series

OTHER TITLES BY RENEE ROSE

Paranormal

Bad Boy Alphas Series

Alpha's Temptation

Alpha's Danger

Alpha's Prize

Alpha's Challenge

Alpha's Obsession

Alpha's Desire

Alpha's War

Alpha's Mission

Alpha's Bane

Alpha's Secret

Alpha's Prey

Alpha's Sun

Shifter Ops

Alpha's Moon

Alpha's Vow

Alpha's Revenge

Wolf Ranch Series

Rough

Wild

Feral

Savage

Fierce

Ruthless

Untamed

Wolf Ridge High Series

Alpha Bully

Alpha Knight

Midnight Doms

Alpha's Blood

His Captive Mortal

Alpha Doms Series

The Alpha's Hunger

The Alpha's Promise

The Alpha's Punishment

Other Paranormal

The Winter Storm: An Ever After Chronicle

Contemporary

Chicago Bratva

"Prelude" in Black Light: Roulette War

The Director

The Fixer

"Owned" in Black Light: Roulette Rematch

The Enforcer

Vegas Underground Mafia Romance

King of Diamonds

Mafia Daddy

Jack of Spades

Ace of Hearts

Joker's Wild

His Queen of Clubs

Dead Man's Hand

Wild Card

Daddy Rules Series

Fire Daddy

Hollywood Daddy

Stepbrother Daddy

Master Me Series

Her Royal Master

Her Russian Master

Her Marine Master

Yes, Doctor

Double Doms Series

Theirs to Punish

Theirs to Protect

Holiday Feel-Good

Scoring with Santa

Saved

Other Contemporary

Renaissance Discipline

ALSO BY LEE SAVINO

Paranormal romance

The Berserker Saga and Berserker Brides (menage werewolves)

These fierce warriors will stop at nothing to claim their mates.

Draekons (Dragons in Exile) with Lili Zander (menage alien dragons)

Crashed spaceship. Prison planet. Two big, hulking, bronzed aliens who turn into dragons. The best part? The dragons insist I'm their mate.

Bad Boy Alphas with Renee Rose (bad boy werewolves)

Never ever date a werewolf.

Tsenturion Masters with Golden Angel

Who knew my e-reader was a portal to another galaxy? Now I'm stuck with a fierce alien commander who wants to claim me as his own.

Contemporary Romance

Royal Bad Boy

I'm not falling in love with my arrogant, annoying, sex god boss. Nope. No way.

Royally Fake Fiancé

The Duke of New Arcadia has an image problem only a fiancé can fix. And I'm the lucky lady he's chosen to play Cinderella.

Beauty & The Lumberjacks

After this logging season, I'm giving up sex. For...reasons.

Her Marine Daddy

My hot Marine hero wants me to call him daddy...

Her Dueling Daddies

Two daddies are better than one.

Innocence: dark mafia romance with Stasia Black

I'm the king of the criminal underworld. I always get what I want. And she is my obsession.

Beauty's Beast: a dark romance with Stasia Black

Years ago, Daphne's father stole from me. Now it's time for her to pay her family's debt...with her body.

ABOUT RENEE ROSE

USA TODAY BESTSELLING AUTHOR RENEE ROSE loves a dominant, dirty-talking alpha hero! She's sold over a million copies of steamy romance with varying levels of kink. Her books have been featured in USA Today's *Happily Ever After* and *Popsugar*. Named Eroticon USA's Next Top Erotic Author in 2013, she has also won *Spunky and Sassy's* Favorite Sci-Fi and Anthology author, *The Romance Reviews* Best Historical Romance, and *has* hit the *USA Today* list seven times with her Wolf Ranch series and various anthologies.

Please follow her on:
  Bookbub | Goodreads

Renee loves to connect with readers!
www.reneeroseromance.com
reneeroseauthor@gmail.com

ABOUT LEE SAVINO

Lee Savino is a USA today bestselling author, mom and chocoholic.

Warning: Do not read her Berserker series, or you will be addicted to the huge, dominant warriors who will stop at nothing to claim their mates.

I repeat: Do. Not. Read. The Berserker Saga. Particularly not the thrilling excerpt below.

Download a free book from www.leesavino.com (don't read that either. Too much hot, sexy lovin').